PROOF O

by

Diana Rock

Thanks for your support!

Diana Rock

Dedication

To Mom with thanks for your love and support
and for instilling a love of baking in my soul.

CHAPTER ONE

Jackie Thorndike hadn't been asked to serve beverages to her boss and the new job applicant. It was simply the nice thing to do. One last task before she finished today's shift. Steadying the tray as she walked, the heavy pitcher of lemonade and two glasses jostled together. Jackie put her back to the swinging kitchen door and gently pushed, entering the sales and eating area of the bakery, where her boss, Jamaica Jones, and the new applicant were sitting.

A tingle ran up Jackie's spine as it always did when she entered this area. It was the same feeling she got the moment in *The Wizard of Oz* when Dorothy opens the door into MunchkinLand, going from black and white into Technicolor. Except there weren't any birds singing or violins playing in Jam Bakery.

In front of the harlequin-pattern tiled walls were wicker baskets for bread, empty now. Also empty were the display cases for colorful pastries and sweets of every kind, when fully stocked. Yet the scent of sugar and yeasty bread still filled the area, making her stomach growl.

The lipstick red awning, along with the sunshine-yellow-painted walls of the bakery made the space bright and cheerful. Far more cheerful than the windowless, dingy gray of the commercial kitchen on the other side of the swinging door, where the temperatures were up to twenty degrees higher than out here when the ovens were in use.

Rounding the corner of the eating area, Jackie caught sight of her boss and the back of the applicant. Jamaica sat uncomfortably at the café table, her pregnant belly taking up all her lap space. Across from her, the new applicant sat stiffly, his forearms resting on the tabletop, his back rigid. When she was within ten feet of them, the man turned his head slightly to look out the window at the sunny mid-May day.

Jackie sucked in a breath and stopped abruptly in her tracks. She knew that profile. She knew that man. Swearing under her breath, she shuffled sideways to turn back, to retreat to the kitchen before she was noticed. The last person she wanted to see applying for the open position was Mark Zutka, and yet here he was doing just that.

Before she could decide, Jamaica noticed her. "Ah, Jackie. Aren't you sweet, bringing us something to drink."

Gingerly turning back to face them, she caught their inquisitive stare. "I, uh, forgot napkins."

Mark Zutka's left eyebrow raised ever so slightly, and a glimmer of surprise grew on his face. Even his eyes seemed to twinkle at her predicament. He folded his hands across his chest and smirked that stupid smirk she'd always hated. The one she'd always wanted to wipe off his face with, oh, the palm of her hand or, at one time, a baseball bat.

Caught, she had no choice but to continue to the café table with the tray. The glasses clinked as she approached. "I thought you might like some refreshment before I left for the day." She eased the tray down to table level.

It was like slow motion. She saw Mark's hand reach out for the nearest glass. Before she could utter a word of warning, he lifted the glass, unbalancing the tray. The tray tipped back toward Jackie. The crystal pitcher tilted sideways, spilling lemonade down the front of her shirt and pants. The cold wetness made her muscles stiffen as the liquid quickly soaked through her thin shirt, running down her abdomen into her pants. Unable to move for fear of dropping the whole tray, she stood still, silently watching as the beverage ran down her legs, pooling on the floor at her feet.

"Oh, Jackie! Oh, dear me. Here, let me help you," Jamaica yelled as she tried to reach over her swollen belly, but the distance was too far. She tried to stand, but her baby bump got in the way, preventing her from providing any assistance.

Mark set the glass in his hand down on the table top and reached out for the pitcher. Nearly empty, he grabbed it off the tilted tray and set it on the table. The tray, unbalanced once again, tipped precipitously, sending the remaining glass to shatter on the floor.

Jackie's arms dropped to her sides, one hand still holding the useless tray. Her eyes surveyed the carnage.

Stepping aside from the mess, she turned her narrowed eyes to Mark. "Thanks! Thanks a lot for that, Mark. If that's the way you intend to act here, you might as well leave now. We don't have time for those kinds of pranks."

"I'm very sorry." Mark scrubbed a hand over his face; his lips pressed tight together.

Jackie felt steam coming out of her ears. *Is he trying not to laugh?*

Jamaica looked from Jackie to Mark, open-mouthed. She blinked. "You two know each other?"

Mark gave a slow nod. "We met at culinary school."

Turning to her boss, Jackie said, "I'm sorry. Stay where you are so you don't slip and fall. I'll clean it up."

Ignoring her, Jamaica gave a guttural sound as she tried to stand up. Liquid was puddling beneath her chair. "Mark, your work history looks good. And your flour milling skills are exactly what we need. You're the only applicant with the right skills. I hate to say this without more questioning, but I have no choice now." Jamaica pressed her hands to her taut abdomen. "Under the immediate circumstances, Mark, you're hired."

Mark and Jackie stared wide-eyed at Jamaica, then at each other.

"Well, don't just stand there. Call Ronnie! My water just broke."

Jackie's eyes widened so large her eyebrows shot up. "B-but you're not due for another two weeks!"

Grasping her swollen abdomen, Jamaica moaned before replying. "Somebody forgot to inform this baby of the timeline."

Mark set his phone down on the table, glancing at the two women. "The ambulance is on its way."

"Jackie, please call Ronnie. If he sees that ambulance pull up outside, he'll freak out."

Doing as she was told, Jackie pulled out her phone. "Ronnie, It's Jackie. Now, don't panic. Nothing's wrong. It's just that Jamaica's water broke. We've called the ambulance. She's sitting down and doing okay—" Before she could say any more, the bakery door slammed open, and Ronnie sprinted across the dining area to his wife's side. "Wow, that was record time," she said, stepping aside.

Mark also stepped away from the table, grabbing his phone. "How'd he get here so fast?" he murmured to Jackie.

Jackie turned her back to the couple to give them some privacy. "He owns the confectionary shop across the street." She pointed out the window at the Fulton's Creamery and Confections diagonally across the street from them.

Mark turned around and looked. The two of them walked to the plate glass window at the front of the bakery. Main Street in the city of Fulton River, Vermont lay before them. Lined with aged red brick two-story buildings erected in the early 1900s, the lower levels held shops with large plate glass windows and narrow wooden doors. Original hardware like brass doorknobs and hinges, gold lettering on the windows, and even canvas awnings and window boxes stuffed with colorful flowers added to the charm.

Even the apartments above the shops still had their decorative wood trims and bold paint schemes from yesteryear. The wooden boardwalk along the shops had deteriorated and been replaced with raised sidewalks years ago. Those raised walkways had helped some businesses survive the hurricane last year.

Jackie turned on him, a forced smile on her face, her teeth clenched tight. "What in God's name are you doing here?"

He raised an eyebrow. "Interviewing for a temporary job baking bread."

"Did you come here to harass me?" The ache in the center of her chest escaping in a hiss, she kept her voice down.

"I didn't know you worked here when I applied." He whispered as they both stepped aside to let the volunteer fire department's ambulance crew into the dining area.

"My name and photo are on the website. You must have seen it."

"I didn't check the website. Frankly, I'm not that fussy about a temp job. I heard about an opening, and I applied. Simple as that."

She scrubbed her face with her hand. Knowing Mark as she did, she knew he was telling the truth. Looking up a possible employer wouldn't have occurred to him, especially if he was hard up for a job. "Between jobs?"

Mark pursed his lips then nodded. "Guess you could say that."

They remained silent as the EMTs settled Jamaica on the gurney and strapped her in. As they wheeled her closer, Jamaica held up her hand to stop them. "Wait a minute."

Ronnie stepped up. "Jam, later."

"Just a minute, Ronnie."

Jamaica waved Jackie over. "I meant to give you some final instructions before I left." She pressed her hand to her belly and winced. "I thought I had a little more time."

"It's okay. It can wait." Jackie patted her boss's shoulder.

"No, it can't. Mark takes over the bread from you. Isabelle can oversee the pastries. I want you to help her as needed, but you are to oversee everything else—front sales room and kitchen."

Jackie's heart stopped beating. She couldn't believe what she was hearing. "I thought I would be in charge of pastries when you left."

"I know. But Isabelle has been helping me these last few months. She knows what to do and how I like things done."

"But—"

"And she's working on a special project for me. For the bakery."

Jackie dropped her eyes to the floor to hide the tears seeping into them.

"Besides, you have to keep the whole operation going. I don't want you confined to any one task while you have so much else to keep track of."

Jamaica grasped her hand to give it a squeeze just as a contraction gripped her. The gentle squeeze to Jackie's hand turned into a near bone-crushing clasp as Jackie yelped in pain and sank to her knees. Ronnie came to her aid, releasing Jamaica's fingers and helping Jackie to her feet.

Huffing from the pain as the contraction subsided, "I'm sorry," Jamaica winced.

Ronnie interrupted, "Jam, let's go."

She shot him a pained look. "Yes, okay. Jackie, take good care of my bakery."

As the gurney and entourage headed for the door, Jackie called out, "Will do, Jam. Don't worry." She smiled as best she could; her heart and spirit splintered from the disappointment of not being able to do what she loved, pastry arts, yet again.

Jackie stood by the front door, watching the ambulance lights disappear down Main Street on the way to Brattleboro Hospital. It was hard for her to tell what emotions were more prominent: the excitement of seeing Jamaica and Ronnie's baby coming into the world, missing the chance to run the pastry section of the bakery yet again, or the anger she felt at Jamaica's having left the task of hiring her temporary replacement until the last possible minute and then giving the job to the first applicant to show up. Serendipity may have placed Mark Zutka in the same bakery she worked in, but it was dumb, stupid bad luck Jamaica had given him the job without so much as the interrogation he deserved. If she had, and if she had spoken to Jackie about him, Jamaica might have thought better of hiring him outright, no matter the haste of the moment.

CHAPTER TWO

I should be grateful she left me in charge of everything. Maybe. The weight of the bakery now rested on Jackie's shoulders for as long as Jamaica was out on maternity leave. It was a feeling she used to think she would enjoy, but it was heavier than she thought. Jamaica hadn't left her totally unprepared. Jackie had been at her side for a year and a half and was familiar with the operation.

Sighing deeply, she turned back into the room and shut the door. Mark sat at a table across the room. Seeing her approach, he stood up.

He eyed her outfit, still damp from the spilled lemonade. "Can I help clean up the mess?" he asked. "Tell me where the dust pan and mop are, and I'll take care of it."

Jackie shook her head, hands on her hips, feet wide apart. "Nothing doing, Mark. Just get the hell out of here. Bad enough I'll have to work with you; you're not starting this minute."

"It's been eight years. Let it go." Mark said.

Jackie jerked backward as if she had been slapped. "Let it go?" she asked. "Let it go. I'm not surprised you want me to forget what you did," she retorted. "But let it go? Never."

"What I did?" Mark glared at her and shook his head before turning away. "That's rich, even for you." He walked back to the interview table, tiptoeing through the broken glass, picked up his folder, and headed for the door. At the threshold, he stopped. "I'll be back tomorrow. What time do I start?"

Arms crossed over her chest, legs planted, Jackie glared back at him.

"What's that? I didn't hear you," Mark cupped his hand to his ear.

Jackie felt the steam spewing out her ears. "Three," she said. "That's in the morning."

Mark gave her a nod and was gone.

Alone in the closed bakery, still fuming over everything that had happened, Jackie began to pace the unaffected black and white tiled floor. *Did he tip that tray intentionally? Had he really not known she worked there?* She chewed on her fingernail. Then she shook her head.

What did it matter? Jamaica had hired him. It was too late to do anything but deal with the consequences of that action.

A crunch underfoot brought Jackie back to the situation at hand. With a sigh, she headed for the mop closet, intent on cleaning up the mess and getting the hell out of the shop. But all the while, her mind worked on how she would handle Mark, the best bread baker in her pastry arts program and her former boyfriend.

***

The familiar log cabin came into view. Mark breathed a sigh as he parked his old Dodge Ram Quad Cab beside the battered Jeep CJ7. *You swore to yourself you'd never return.* He cut his pickup's engine and sat staring at the grayed logs stacked so precisely. The only sign of life was the light smoke seeping from the chimney top. That and the presence of his brother's Jeep gave evidence Joe was home. Mark sucked in a deep breath, grabbed his duffel bag, and headed for the heavy wooden front door.

The side of his fist hit the solid oak with a thud. Mark winced and frowned as he rubbed his hand. His eyes searched for a doorbell. None. Several more times he struck the door, each time feeling his blood pressure increase in proportion to the pain level in his hand.

The door cracked open a couple inches.

"Joey, it's me." Mark called out as he tried to shove his hiking-boot-clad foot between the door and the jamb.

"No. Not again." Joe's voice whined as he tried to slam the door shut. But Mark's hand and boot tip prevented it.

"It's temporary."

The two brothers wrestled with the door until Mark threw all his bulk against it, knocking Joe aside and the door open. He skirted past his brother, lying on the floor shaking his head.

"Why do you always end up here? Why my place? You have another brother and a married sister. What's wrong with their houses?" Joe argued as he got to his feet and followed Mark into the living space of the one-room cabin. "You know there's no space for you here."

Mark dropped his duffel bag beside the couch and sat down. His head drooping, eyes closed. "That was six months ago when I stayed here. I'm working downtown."

Leaning against the couch, Joe crossed his arms over his chest. "You found a job in Fulton River? I thought you were working in the Berkshires somewhere, grinding grain or some such."

"I was milling fresh flour from fresh grain and making bread with it." Mark scratched the nape of his neck. "It's my skill. My career."

"You call baking bread a skill?"

Mark's eyes narrowed and his lips pinched. He stomped into Joey's kitchen, crashed around searching in cupboards until he returned with a bag of flour and a glass of water. He held both out. "If it's so easy, bro, go for it. Make a loaf of bread. I'll wait."

"Don't be ridiculous."

"I'm not the one who's being ridiculous. I spent a lot of money learning professional and commercial baking. And a lot of years honing that craft."

"So, what happened. With the last job?"

"It ended as it always does." Mark shrugged and flopped against the couch back.

His brother raised his hands pleadingly to heaven before dropping them again. "Jesus, Mark. When are you going to learn? You can't walk in and change things to your liking. Not when you're the low man on the totem pole." When he got the one-finger salute from Mark, Joe walked away.

"I didn't like the rules. And it got boring. So shoot me."

"You're just like Dad. Always looking to be the boss and getting fired for it. Sound familiar?"

Scowling, Mark brought the flour and water back to the kitchen. "I try to make things better. They don't understand my motive is in their best interest." He returned with two beers, handing one to Joey. "I realize I'm homeless yet again. But I don't have his alcohol abuse issues."

Joe eyed the beers and gave his brother a stink eye. "Are you sure?" Then broke out a smirk.

"I'm not the one with a fridge full of beer."

"I work in a brewery, and I get a discount. Answer the question."

"Yeah, I'm sure." Mark stared at his bottle a second before he set it down on the nearest end table. When Joe didn't respond, Mark added, "It's temporary."

"What? Your stay? Hell yeah!"

"Well, yes that, and the job too. It's only six to eight weeks."

"Don't you own a tent? Can't you live in that for the duration since it's temporary?"

"It's buried in my storage unit with everything else I own. I forgot to take it out before I moved my apartment contents into the unit."

Joe rolled his eyes. "And if you don't find something else when it's over?" He crossed his arms over his chest again and waited.

"Have some faith, would ya?"

Joe paced from wall to wall. "Faith? You want me to have faith?" His voice rose an octave at the question. "In you? The only thing I can reasonably have faith in is that you'll end up on my doorstep again looking for a place to stay." He stopped in front of the kitchen sink and stared out the window. "And that you'll stay longer than you let on."

Mark's already heavy heart sank deeper. Joe was right. He'd stayed here far more often than he wanted. But he couldn't keep a job only for a paycheck. Maybe half the population could do that, blindly go to work at a job they despised, working with people they loathed, for bosses they hated. He wasn't one of them. He wanted respect. Respect for his skills, his knowledge, and his work. And a paycheck to match—with benefits. He desperately wanted benefits.

As if reading his thoughts, Joe asked, "Could this go permanent?"

"Maybe. I'm covering for someone on maternity leave."

"So, if she doesn't come back?"

"Yeah, I thought of that. I could be hired on to stay."

"Bennies?"

"Vacation, holiday, and sick time paid. No insurance or pension. Not for temporary or part-time staff."

Joe hitched his head. "Well, it's an improvement over your last job's benefits."

"What benefits?" Mark smirked.

Laughing, Joe nodded. "Exactly my point." He looked at his brother thoughtfully. "Go on, settle in. You know where." He grabbed Mark's arm and got nose to nose with him. "This is the last time, man. You're my brother and I love you, but this has to stop. There will not be an open door next time."

"Thanks bro, you're the best." He clapped Joe on the shoulder, picked up his duffel bag, and headed for the loft ladder.

"Oh, one more thing" Joe grabbed his arm, stopping him. "I have a hot date Saturday night. Make yourself scarce that night. Capisce?"

"All night?"

"If a red bandanna is hanging on the outside doorknob, I don't want you inside this cabin until noon the next day. Or I'll reconsider our arrangement."

"Right."

Mark climbed the ladder to the loft. The space was so small he couldn't even stand. Crawling on the rough-hewn pine boards on his hands and knees, he tucked his bag beneath the window. An old pool raft lay deflated where he'd left it last time he was here. After wiping the dust off the valve stem with his sleeve, he blew it up, only to have it deflate as soon as he sat on it. *Purchase number one: new inflatable pool raft.*

CHAPTER THREE

When Jackie turned off the automatic mixer kneading the rye bread dough, she heard the telephone ring. She glanced at her watch. It was 3:32 am. First day of work and he was late. She sighed heavily, her eyes blurry and her patience thin from not enough sleep. How could she sleep after all the upsets that had transpired in the last twenty-four hours? Jamaica going into labor two weeks early.

Jackie didn't know much about being pregnant, but she knew early deliveries were not a good thing. Plus, she didn't get put in charge of pastries like she wanted, she was now responsible for the entire bakery. Everything from staff to purchasing supplies, maintaining stock, quality control, scheduling. About the only thing she didn't have to do was write paychecks though she would have to call in hours to the accountant. And this instantaneous hiring of Mark Zutka.

It had taken years to get over the sorrow and humiliation of what happened between them eight years ago. In all that time, she hadn't seen or heard from him after he walked out on her. Now she was supposed to teach him the bread baking schedule and supervise him until Jamaica came back? If she came back? After wiping her floury hands, she flung the dish towel over her left shoulder and answered the phone trying to keep the fury out of her voice. "Jam Bakery."

"Are you going to open the door and let me in or let me stand here another half-hour?" Mark's voice bellowed through the receiver.

"You haven't been waiting outside for half an hour, I've been checking the door, waiting for you." The flare of anger rose up in her gut, flying out in her tone.

"Did you check the front door?" Mark drawled.

Jackie sighed, furious with herself. No, she hadn't been checking the front door of the bakery. She'd assumed he would park behind the building and seek entry through the back door. "Hang on; I'll be right there."

She yanked the towel off her shoulder and slammed it onto the stainless-steel table top as she put down the phone. Striding through the swinging doors brought her into the sales part of the bakery. There, silhouetted at the door by the moonlight, was Mark Zutka. *Damn!*

A quick walk across the shop brought her to the door. "You're late," she said through the glass door. She stood with her arms crossed over her chest, her weight balanced solidly between both her feet.

"On the contrary," he replied, "I've been standing here for thirty minutes. Are you going to open the door, or not?"

Jackie flipped the deadbolt and gave the door a shove.

Mark caught it as it flew open before it could smack into the side of the building.

"Follow me." Jackie led him behind the sales counter to the door of the kitchen. She eyed him up and down. "In the future, wear street clothes to work. We change into our working clothes here so as not to contaminate our food products."

Mark smirked. "You're kidding."

"No, I'm not joking. We change here. If you don't like it, you don't have to work here," she reminded him. Jackie led him into the back of the kitchen to the far wall containing several doors. "The far-right door is the changing room. The next door over is the bathroom. The door beside that is the mop closet."

"For today, we'll overlook the shop policy," she said, eying his chef's uniform of white double-breasted jacket and hounds-tooth-patterned, black and white pants. "Also, we don't go much for traditional chef's attire. Comfortable pants and tee shirts mainly with large white aprons while we bake. We have jackets for when we go out front."

"Can't I wear whatever I want?" Mark asked.

"Sure—knock yourself out. Just thought you'd like to stay comfortable. But no toques. Definitely no toques."

Jackie took a left, walking along the far wall to a door in the corner. She opened it and stepped in, turning on the light. "The pantry," she said, gesturing with her hand to the shelving that lined the walls of the room. Large plastic bins filled the center area of the room. "Any dry item can be found here." She pointed to a side room that held stacks of fifty-pound bags of grains, "This is the grain and flour room. We keep it temperature controlled. We use ten different types of flour in our goods. We mill most of our own flour. But we do purchase a few already milled." Jackie looked at Mark, who gave a nod as they left the room.

She continued walking, waving her hand to the left— "mixers, dough sheeter, dough slicer, fryers" and to the right— "proofers and the ovens." In between were four eight-foot-long stainless-steel tables, a marble-topped table, and a wood-topped table, as well as rolling racks for holding baked goods ready for packaging. Along one wall space were shelves holding bakeware, pan racks, and boxes of assorted plastic bags and bakery boxes for packaging baked goods. In one corner stood stainless-steel triple-basin industrial sinks for washing, rinsing, and sterilizing all the bakeware and equipment.

"Neat place. Small but everything we need to get the products out," she said. "In addition to supplying our storefront with products, we have ten commercial contracts, providing grinder rolls, cakes, and dinner rolls for local restaurants."

Mark nodded, taking it all in. Already there were bakery products in various stages of completion. A two-gallon bucket of egg wash sat on a table, a paint brush beside it. Floured cloths for baguettes hung on racks and wood handled razor blades called lames for cutting designs in the tops of bread loaves sat in plastic bins, safely out of the way.

He's too quiet. Something must be up. "Any questions? Concerns?"

"No—not just yet," Mark said, then bit his lip. "Actually, what are my hours going to be?"

"I'll be taking Jamaica's hours during her absence: five am until two pm. And you're taking mine—which means three in the morning to eleven-thirty. You get a half-hour for breakfast. Sometime between six and seven. We don't have set times for coffee breaks. When the product's baking, we might grab a cup and put our feet up for a few minutes unless there's something else pressing to do." Jackie walked back to the center table. "You'll be responsible for making all breads, rolls, and muffins. When that's done, you help me," she explained. "We are open to customers from six until three. Jenny, Vanessa, and Isabelle work the front."

"What do you do?" Mark asked, leaning his hip against the table, and crossing his arms over his chest.

"Isabelle and I make pretty much everything else. Breakfast pastry, cookies, brownies, cakes, and pies."

"If I remember correctly, that was your specialty at culinary school—pastries and cakes."

A loud buzzer sounded from the proofer.

"Time to pop the white bread in the oven," she said, reaching for the hand mitts. She deftly moved a large tray of loaf pans to the oven beside the proofer and set the timer.

"What's next?" Mark asked.

"I have a whiteboard list hanging on the wall over there." She pointed to it. "Rye bread dough needs to be kneaded and measured into loaf pans." Jackie didn't stop moving. "Let's get cracking."

Mark paused to read the whiteboard. The list was extensive. She ignored him, moving on to the dough slicer.

"One question." Mark called out.

Pausing before she started weighing out the rye bread dough, a dough knife in hand, Jackie gave him her attention though her gut churned. She had a feeling what was coming. "What?"

"I don't see any sourdough on the list. Don't you make sourdough bread here?" The corners of his mouth edged up, a smirk in the making.

The top of Jackie's head felt like it was going to blow off and she gripped the knife hard, trying to overpower the urge to throw it at him. Glaring and icy, she replied, "We. Don't. Do. Sourdough."

Mark's face broke into a full sneer.

Jackie's feet launched her in his direction, the knife still gripped in her hand. Mark's eyes bulged with fear as she advanced his way.

The shrill ringing of the phone stopped Jackie and Mark in their tracks.

Jackie hustled over to the phone stand and picked up the portable device from its charger. "Hello?"

"Jackie? It's Ronnie. It's a girl! Jamaica had a baby girl!" said the proud father.

"Oh my God, Ronnie, that's wonderful! How is everyone doing? Is Jamaica okay? What about the baby?" Jackie set down the knife, her entire body and disposition relaxing.

"Everyone is doing fine. She's cute as a button! Blue hair and blond eyes. I can't wait to show her off," Ronnie Caswell said.

Jackie laughed at his verbal mix-up and beamed, "I'm so happy for you both. Give my love to Jamaica. Tell her everything is fine here and not to worry."

"Sure thing. Got to go. More people to call, you know how it is."

"Okay, goodbye."

Clicking the phone off, Jackie turned toward Mark. "So, it's a girl. Everyone is fine."

"Great to hear," Mark said, shifting his weight between his two feet ever so slightly as if he was unsure if he should still run and hide or if the crisis was over.

Jackie set the phone down on the small desk beside the door to the sales room. "Okay, that phone call reminds me. If the phone rings before we open at six, let it roll to the answering machine. If for some reason you do answer it and it's an order, write it down and place it on the order clipboard hanging on the far wall over there." She pointed to the clipboard. "Now, let's get cracking," she said sternly. "And no more wise cracks about sourdough bread."

***

Jackie sat at the back corner table in the bakery's dining area. Sun didn't penetrate this far back, leaving her sitting in gloomy darkness. On the table before her was an empty coffee cup and plate and a pile of napkin pieces.

A shadow crossed over the table, startling her. Looking up, she found Regina Maxwell, owner and floral designer of Gina Blooms.

"My goodness, you are far away, girlfriend. Mind if I crash your party?" Regina didn't wait for an answer. She sat down, dropping her purse on the table alongside her coffee cup and a chocolate croissant. Gesturing with her chin, "What's the confetti for?"

"I'm just thinking. And making a mess." Jackie scooped the napkin bits onto her empty plate.

"You look like you've lost hope," Gina said before taking a bit of croissant. She closed her eyes. "Mmmm, these are so good."

Jackie sniffled and wiped at the moisture forming in her eyes. "I'm feeling stuck in a rut. And I don't know what to do about it."

"Work-related?" she said between mouthfuls of croissant.

"Yeah." Jackie stretched her neck and searched past her friend to see if anyone else was around to hear the conversation. There was no one else, but Jackie lowered her voice anyhow. "When I took this job, it was with the understanding that I would start off running the breads and then as the business grew, transition to assistant pastry chef."

"You made Jamaica's wedding cake and all those delicious hors d'oeuvre, didn't you?"

"I did. I wanted to show Jamaica and everyone else what I could do." Jackie fingered the pile of napkin bits on her plate. "Instead, Jamaica asked someone else to help do pastries. No promotion for me."

Wiping her fingers on a napkin, Regina was thoughtful. "I see. Did you talk to her?"

"I tried when it first happened. She said I was doing a spectacular job at breads, and she didn't want to have to train someone new on breads. It's quite intensive between the flour milling and everything. So, she's got Isabelle to help her in the morning before she goes out front to the sales room for the rest of her shift."

"What's the plan with Jamaica on maternity leave?"

Jackie closed her eyes and mashed her lips together. "She's put me in charge of the bakery while she's gone."

Her friend's eyes widened. "Wow! That's quite an honor."

"It's quite a headache. Just before she left, she hired someone to cover bread baking, to free me up to oversee everything. But there's a complication. He and I used to be —"

Regina's mouth dropped open and her eyes nearly bugged out of her head. "No way! You've got to be kidding me."

"I wish I was." She shrugged, a combination smirk and frown on her face. "It didn't end well at all. And now we have to deal with each other. No, worse. I have to oversee him. But what can I do? I can't leave Jamaica in a lurch. She doesn't know about the history between Mark and myself and I'd like to keep it that way."

Regina eyed her gravely. "Are you thinking of leaving?"

"I am, but I'm torn. I really love Jam Bakery and this little town. I could go back to the city. But I'm enjoying the quiet and calm of the country. I grew up not far from here."

"Boston's a good place. You worked there before, right?"

"I did. Six years at the best bakery in Beantown. Joanne would hire me back in a heartbeat. She told me that when I left."

Regina smirked. "There's a lot more eligible men in Boston."

"For sure! This place is a dating desert." Jackie heaved a sigh. "I don't want to move back there. I really want to stay in Vermont."

"Did you have your first baking class yet with the adult education group at the high school?"

Her face broke into a smile. "I've had several. Jamaica didn't even want to start the classes. I just substituted for her from the beginning. It's kind of fun. They're a good bunch. Most of the class has some baking experience. But there are a couple of men that are testing my will to succeed."

"I think it's a brilliant idea. But when do you sleep?" Regina chuckled.

Jackie shrugged, rubbing her eyes. "That's the problem, I don't! And you wonder why I'm feeling edgy and depressed."

"Maybe something will come up."

Jackie cocked her head. "You mean like something will materialize out of thin air, so to speak?"

"Well, yeah. If you concentrate on what you're needing, maybe the universe will deliver."

"Ha!" Jackie scoffed at the very idea. "Sorry, I don't go for that mumbo-jumbo and hocus pocus." She stood up and reached for her dirty dishes.

"Suit yourself." Regina smiled over the rim of her coffee cup. "But what do you have to lose?"

CHAPTER FOUR

It was eight-fifteen, and Jackie was finally getting her morning breakfast break. Despite her irritation with Mark being late yesterday, he had managed to arrive on time today and work hard for the last five hours. He followed her directions without question and managed to stick to the list of tasks well enough that Jackie felt comfortable leaving him alone in the kitchen for half an hour.

She tried not to think about all the trouble he could be causing as she sipped her morning French Roast coffee and nibbled at her croissant breakfast sandwich. Silently and leisurely, she thumbed through a bakery association newsletter. It listed the openings and closings of bakeries and bakery-cafes in the state of Vermont, among other things. This month's edition had an article on a bakery in Burlington specializing in items made with fresh herbs. Jackie skimmed it, not finding it of much interest.

She perused the rest of the newsletter, finally getting to the last page. This was her personal favorite. It listed job openings and who just got hired where. Jackie liked to keep track of her former culinary school classmates.

Suddenly she was choking on a sip of coffee, nearly spewing it out her nose. There, in the job openings section, was a listing for her dream job. King Mills Flour Company's baking school was looking for a baking instructor.

A shuffling noise heading her way forewarned of Mark's approach. She set the paper down and turned toward him. "What?"

"I need to show you something." He crooked his finger at her, beckoning her to follow.

Frowning, she got up and followed.

Jackie halted in the door of the storage room. "What's the problem?" Her arms planted on her hips; and her eyes narrowed as she looked around for something out of place.

Mark pointed to the temperature gauge on the far wall. "It's too warm in here."

Jackie glanced up. It was sixty degrees. Two degrees above the top end of the range set in the bakery's standard operating procedure. Jackie rolled her eyes. *If this is what Mark called a major problem, what would he call a catastrophe?*

Mark's face darkened. "Don't give me that. You know grains mill better when they're colder. And since we're on the subject, that range of forty to fifty-eight degrees isn't adequate. Above fifty degrees, any insect larva in the grain can flourish. Keep it below fifty and they remain dormant."

Advancing into the room, Jackie stopped before the nearest bin of soft white wheat berries. "I can't keep it so cold in here it detrimentally affects other ingredients."

Sweeping his arm over the expanse of shelving along the walls, he asked, "Show me one — just one that would be—" and he raised the first two fingers of each hand to make air quotes, "detrimentally affected."

Rounding on him, she got into his personal space. "Look. I don't need to explain our ways to you. They are what they are. Accept them, work within them, or leave." She spun on her heels and headed for the door.

Mark's voice called out. "Have you ever tried doing sprouted flour?"

She stopped in her tracks, her heart pounding, the steam rolling through her veins. She had done some milling of sprouted grains a long time back during her internship at Berkshire Breads. When she first started at Jam Bakery, she had intended to discuss adding it to their menu. But shortly after opening the bakery, Jamaica and Ronnie had their wedding and she had concentrated on making their wedding cake and hors d'oeuvres. And then, somehow, she had forgotten all about it.

Mark broke into her thoughts. "People with gut issues prefer it. It has 25% less carbs, 40% less fat, 47% less gluten and a lower lectin content. Also, -"

"I know all that. I'll think about it." She rubbed her forehead.

"The process is easy; it just takes a few extra days. But the health benefits make it a quick sell."

Jackie glared at him. "It's not my bakery. I'd have to run it through Jamaica."

"But it's a good idea." Mark's eyebrow cocked up slightly.

What the hell does he want? A blessed medal? Jackie sighed. "Not a bad idea." *Especially since it was my idea first.*

"So, you'll take it up with Jamaica?"

Her face flushed and hardened. "Jamaica has her hands full with a newborn infant. She's out on leave for the next six to eight weeks. I am not going to spring this idea on her now." She lowered her tone of voice from the shrill it was to a more normal tone. "Even if I did, she'd want a full market analysis. Between the bakery and teaching, I don't have time to prepare one."

Mark fisted his hands on his hips. "I'll do it."

Jackie couldn't help the flaring anger raging throughout her body. He was not going to leave it be. But it was her idea. And this upstart, a temporary worker, Mark Zutka, of all people, was going to steal her spotlight? Not a chance. She knew how to play the game. "Fine. If you want to write it up and give it to me, I'll pass it to Jamaica when she's back to work."

"But I'll be gone when she comes back." Mark reminded her.

Her smile and tone saccharine sweet, "I know."

***

Days later, Jackie reviewed the lesson plan one last time. The lesson was simple and straightforward: how to make different pastries with commercially purchased puff pastry dough. The students in the adult education class should be able to finish the lesson easily within the two-hour time frame. Getting out on time was always a problem with her class. It was hard to get all the baking and cleaning up done in time to leave within the two-hour window. But it was imperative to leave on time, not just to lock up the school by nine-fifteen.

She also needed to get home and grab another five hours of sleep before her work shift started. Until Mark was comfortable working on his own at three in the morning, she would have to come in with him instead of coming in later at five. She couldn't wait for the day when she could sleep in until four after a teaching night.

Next, she reviewed the supplies list. She had everything on the list at home, ready for class. If she got to the high school home economics classroom half an hour before class began, the dough would have enough time to thaw.

Jackie itched to get back into the classroom to instruct the eager students in the baking class. This was her first-time teaching baking arts, and she loved it. It was fun to watch them get it right and fun to watch them make the same beginner mistakes she had made years ago when she was first learning. She smiled, thinking of the cookies with one tablespoon of salt instead of one teaspoon made by one gentleman during the first class. So far, it was only mistakes like that. No one had set fire to anything. Yet.

"Whatcha doing?" Mark asked, coming over to the small kitchen table.

Jackie gathered the papers together and shoved them into her oversized handbag. But several fell loose, floating out across the floor, landing three feet away near Mark. He picked one up.

Mark looked at her, his head cocked to the side. "Lesson five: Puff Pastries?"

Jackie snatched the paper out of his hand and shoved it into her bag. "None of your business."

"No, really. I'm interested. Are you taking a class?" he asked, then shook his head. "That doesn't make any sense. You already know what to do with puff pastries." His eyebrows came together as he scowled in thought.

Jackie gulped down the last of her coffee.

"If you're not taking a class, maybe you're giving a class," he said, slowly reasoning it out.

"What's it to you?" Jackie replied.

"Nothing. I find it interesting, that's all." He pulled out a chair and sat down. "Where do you teach?"

"At the local high school. It's a community education class," she said as she stood up to leave. "The bakery foots some the cost of ingredients, and each student gets an apron with the Jam Bakery logo on it."

Mark's eyebrows raised. "Was this your idea?"

"Actually, it was supposed to be Jamaica's class. She signed up to do it six months ago thinking she'd be done with the class before the baby was born. But by the time class started, she was much too exhausted by her pregnancy to do it, so she asked me to step in as instructor."

Mark looked incredulous. "Why would you teach people to bake if you own a bakery?"

"What's wrong with teaching the locals how to bake simple items?"

"Nothing, except it could keep them baking their own rather than buying here. You know, sabotaging the business."

Jackie turned to face him. "I hardly think learning how to make homemade napoleons will hurt our business since we don't sell napoleons."

Mark tapped the table top with his index finger. "Maybe not napoleons. But what do you teach them that we sell?"

Bending over to look him in the eyes, Jackie said, "I don't teach them to make anything that they can buy here except for a type of cinnamon bread." She wasn't going to tell him that the students were now frequent customers and the result had been an uptick in sales. The less she spoke with him the better.

Mark was silent as he stared into Jackie's eyes.

A shiver went zipping up Jackie's spine as she watched his brown eyes watching her. He really did have lovely eyes for a guy. She stood up, turned, and walked back into the kitchen area to begin packaging the now cooled grinder rolls.

Mark picked up the other paper she had left on the floor. It was a brochure about Groton State Forest. He folded it in half and stuffed it in his back pocket. *Might be an interesting place to mountain bike on the Memorial Day holiday coming up.*

CHAPTER FIVE

It had been good to hang out at the Whiskey Den for the first time in a year or so, Mark mused as he steered his truck down the dirt road to Joe's cabin. He'd put in his week of work and rewarded himself with a night out. Though he'd felt perfectly fine when he left the place, he was now feeling a little tipsy. He'd worked that morning and had no sleep since 2 am, so his lightheaded feeling probably had more to do with lack of sleep than the three beers he drank. All the same, he was thankful there hadn't been any DUI check points along the half-mile route from the bar to the dirt road.

Joe's Jeep stood in the driveway. *Thought he'd be out carousing tonight.* It wasn't terribly late, just before midnight. After parking beside the Jeep, he headed for the front door. Fumbling with the key, he found the door unlocked. *Hmm, Joe must have fallen asleep watching TV.* Quietly, he entered the cabin so as not to wake his brother.

The wood stove was going, its front doors open, and in their place was a screen. The firelight cast a glaze of orange light onto a naked couple in the middle of the floor, on the bear skin rug, in the midst of intercourse. The sight sobered Mark up quickly. Frozen in place, he assessed his options. He couldn't cross the room to escape up the ladder to the loft without being seen. And he might get caught opening the front door again if he tried to slip out. He turned his back on the preoccupied couple, raised his hands to cover his ears from the moans and squeals, and dropped his keys on the entry's flagstone floor with a crash,

He glanced over his shoulder when all vocalizations ceased. All motion had ceased as well.

"What was that?" a female voice whispered on the loud side.

Joe's voice replied, "I don't know. Let me get the light."

Mark closed his eyes and covered them with his hand, shaking his head. "It's me. I'm not looking."

The female yelped, and scurrying sounds followed along with the rumpling of clothes. "Mark?" Joe called out.

"Yeah."

Whispering between the couple was indistinguishable except for its heated tone.

"Mark?"

"Yeah?" Mark replied, knowing what was coming.

"Get the fuck out of here."

"Right." Mark picked up his fallen keys and stumbled out the front door. *Shit.* His mind jogged about, giving him a fuzzy memory of Joe saying he had a date Saturday night. *It's Saturday, all right. Double Shit.* Wasn't Joe going to hang something on the doorknob? He hadn't seen or felt anything on it. But he hadn't looked for anything either.

When Mark shut the door behind him, he double-checked the knob. There wasn't anything there. Pulling out his cell phone, he turned on the flashlight. Beside the front step was a red bandanna. Mark pressed his lips together, shook his head, and walked back to his truck. With nowhere else to go, he stretched out across the front bench seat, bunching up an old hoodie for a pillow.

The cabin door slamming made his eyes pop open again. As did the yelling.

"That's my brother. He's not all that ... together. What am I supposed to do? Kick him out? Come on, Michelle. Don't be like that."

"Are you going to take me home, or do I have to walk the entire way?" Joe's date yelled back as she marched toward the dirt road.

Keeping his head down, Mark counted the seconds, knowing the longer Joe took to reply, the worse it was going to be.

"FINE!" Michelle's scream and the grating sound of her footsteps in the pea gravel of the driveway faded.

Mark heard his brother slam the front door shut again. "Fuck! Wait! I'll drive you."

Nestling back down onto the bench seat, Mark closed his eyes and listened as heavy footfalls came closer.

A smash of breaking glass and a shower of shards jolted him upright. "Shit! What the flyin-"

Joe stuck his head in the space where Mark's passenger window used to be. "You—thanks for ruining a perfectly good night with Michelle. I thought I told you to stay away tonight. Didn't you see the signal?"

"Sorry bro, the signal wasn't there. It must have fallen off."

"Sorry doesn't cut it." Joe got in his Jeep, peeled out of the driveway with stones flying, in pursuit of his date.

Mark got up gingerly, trying not to cut himself on the shards of safety glass. Getting out of the truck, he inspected the missing window area. *Maybe I should fix it with plastic tonight?* He started for the cabin. *Fuck it.* The last thing he wanted was to still be within earshot or reach of Joe when he came back. Because Mark had a feeling, his mood wasn't going to be any better when he returned.

He got back in his truck and drove to the only place he could think of to park. The parking lot behind Jam Bakery held a few scattered cars along the far edge. Probably vehicles owned by the tenants of apartments on the second and third stories above the shops. Shutting off the truck, he sat, his hands gripping the steering wheel, staring off into the sky.

What the hell am I doing? What the hell has happened with my life? His eyes burned. Closing them, he pondered where he went wrong. He'd had it all together after high school. He knew exactly what he wanted to do. Hell, he knew even before then.

Back when he was a kid, watching his grandma make bread. He'd been mesmerized how she put a pile of flour on the table, added a little salt and water and yeast to a well in the center and pulled it all together into a dough. Every evening, after dinner, she'd put the dough together, then set it in the fridge to proof overnight. The next morning, fresh baked bread would be on the kitchen table with homemade jam.

As Mark grew older, he was allowed to help, until he was old enough to do it for her. He'd loved the elasticity of the dough as he kneaded it and the heat it generated in his body.

And he loved that fresh bread smell. For him there was no smell better in the world. When Grandma died, every loaf he made was an act of love for her.

It was a no brainer becoming a baker. He'd footed the cost of baking school with student loans he'd yet to finish paying off. The professional baking and pastry arts program had been everything he wanted and more. It sparked a talent he didn't realize he had. He'd soaked up all the information and skills he could.

An image of Jackie flickered through his brain. The first time he met her. The first time he kissed her. The first time they made love. He'd been on top of the world back then. Powered by love and knowledge, he was invincible.

And then, it had gone sour. Over sourdough.

And now here he was, after yet another job loss, bunking in his brother's cabin loft yet again, his worldly goods in storage yet again, working with the woman who popped the dream bubble that sent him in to this six-year freefall.

Mark sighed heavily, the feeling of slumber creeping over him. Using his jacket as a pillow, he leaned against his door and closed his eyes. He needed a plan. He needed to get his shit together. No more seat of his pants, day-by-day living. Tomorrow he'd figure it all out.

As he fell asleep, his mind sank into the happy times it always did just before he drifted off to sleep. The senses of Jackie: asleep in his arms as he spooned her lithe body, the scent of her hair in his nostrils, and his hand cupping her breast.

***

A sharp rapping sound beside his ear jolted Mark upright. Through blurry eyes, he squinted against the morning sun. Another knocking sound brought his attention to the figure on the outside of his truck door.

"What do you want, Thorn?" He scrubbed at his eyes trying to get them to focus better.

"What the hell do you think you're doing here?" Her eyes flashed as the wind caught her dark brown hair, lifting it to swirl about her head. She looked different. Was that makeup on her face?

"I was sleeping." He rolled down the window to talk with her. "What's the problem? It's not my day to work. And what did you do to your face?"

"It's called makeup. I went to church." Scowling, hands on her hips, she took a step away from the vehicle. "God, you smell horrid. Go on a bender last night? Couldn't find your way home?"

"Can it, Thornbush. None of your business."

"Look. If you're an alcoholic that is my business."

"Bullshit. If I'm not sober at work, sure. But what I do on my time is my business."

Jackie glared at him, then her eyes softened. "Why don't you go inside and use the locker room shower. You'll feel better."

"I have a place to stay and shower." *Or I did until last night.* "I'll just go home now."

Without a wave or backward glance Mark rolled up the window, started the truck and left.

On the dirt road to Joe's cabin, he pulled over. He pulled down his visor and checked his face in the mirror. The image staring back at him was his dad. His dad the way he looked the morning after one of his benders. Sunken eye sockets, red, blood-shot, puffy eyes, hair sticking up every which way, a scruff of a beard. Mark slapped the visor away, cursing what he saw. His gut ached from the booze and the lack of food, and his chest started to heave as tears flooded his eyes. *I don't want to be like him.* "I. Don't. Want. To. End. Up. Like. Him." He hissed through his clenched teeth; his knuckles whitening as his hands clutched the steering wheel. He knew he was acting like his father, and he wasn't proud of it.

He was less proud Jackie had found him in his post-inebriated state. It would be the last time. Step number one for getting his life back in order meant limiting his alcohol intake. No more binge drinking because he had nothing better to do and felt sorry for himself. "From now on, you're —" He paused, his brain searching for a reasonable target. "You're only allowed one drink a day."

CHAPTER SIX

A bead of sweat rolled into Mark's eye, causing a stinging sensation. He grabbed the collar of his tee-shirt and pressed it to the pained orb. He knew he was out of shape, but he hadn't realized how much so until this game of basketball. The pick-up game was sponsored by the adult education program at the Fulton River High School gym every Tuesday night.

Feeling the need for a workout, Mark had shown up to join the game. Within minutes he'd regretted his decision. All the other guys not only knew each other, they clearly had been doing this for a while. They had no problem running back and forth the length of the court.

Mark wished he could say the same. Fact was, he spent more time bent over with his hands on his knees, catching his breath than running the ball down the court. By this, the end of the game, he was toast. He shook hands with the rest of the guys and walked back to the locker room. He thought of the shower and how good it was going to feel after such a workout.

As he walked to the locker room door, he caught a whiff of something. The odor of baking bread. His mind reeled with the scent. Cinnamon bread. Maybe with raisins — he couldn't tell. He followed his nose. It led him out into the corridor and down a hallway lined with lockers. It led him to an open-doored classroom. He stepped just inside the threshold and stopped short.

There at the front of the class, in the midst of giving instructions on bread variations, looking relaxed and confident, was Jackie Thorndike. She stood before the fifteen students, holding up a sheet of paper.

"— so instead of cinnamon and raisins, you could put together a mixture of dried herbs, work them into the dough at step three for easy incorporation. Everything is explained on the worksheet," she said, giving the paper a gentle shake.

She startled when she saw Mark in the doorway. She stopped as if unsure whether to say anything or not. Then she said, "Can I help you?"

"No, I smelled the bread and followed my nose. It smells great," he said, suddenly aware of sixteen pairs of eyes upon him. He fidgeted with his hands as he started to back out the doorway. "I thought you were making puff pastries tonight."

Jackie's eyes widened as she stared at him. "That's lesson five. We're doing lesson four tonight, thank you."

Mark could tell she was clenching her teeth as she replied. "I'm sorry to intrude. I guess I'll be going." He turned around and began jogging back to the locker room door. Whatever possessed him to go there in the first place. He should have known it was Jackie's baking class. *I never should have interrupted the class.*

***

Mark stuck his head around the corner of the doorway from the sales area. "Jack—phone," he barked and disappeared.

Jackie jumped in her seat, then sneered, "Jack, phone." She threw down the magazine on the table top before getting up and heading for the office.

She wasn't gone more than two minutes when Mark came back to the table. He pulled back the chair and sat, picking up the magazine after setting down his cup of coffee. Leisurely, he thumbed through the pages, stopping here and there to read a few lines or check out a photo.

He got to the back listing of job openings. As he read, he sipped his java. His eyes caught on one listing. The job listing for King Mills Flour Company. He glanced over both his shoulders to ascertain he was alone. Straightening the paper, he leaned over to take a closer look.

Hot damn! KMF is hiring an instructor. They have terrific bennies. As a young boy he'd seen and experienced what severe medical issues could do to a family: its finances, its cohesion, its future. As he grew into a man, medical insurance was one of those career benefits he needed to feel comfortable, to feel secure. His mind raced into hyper-speed. *Great, I just started my new job, and here's my perfect job now. Too bad they want teaching experience. Where the hell can I get experience?*

He sipped at his coffee cup twice, his mind still regurgitating the information. Then it hit him. Adult-ed classes. Maybe he could get a job teaching an adult-ed class. But it was mid-semester. It might be another six weeks or more before new classes started, and he didn't have that much time. He needed experience for his resume, and he needed it now.

Then it dawned on him. He didn't need his own class. *Maybe I could get Jackie to let me help her with her class. I'd be able to prove I have experience. I'll have to broach this subject with caution. Not scare her with the idea.*

Draining the last of his coffee, he stared at the job listing, memorizing the information. When he heard Jackie's footsteps coming toward the doorway, he closed the magazine and set it down. With the URL memorized, he'd look up the information on his laptop when he got home and work up a resume again. And when the time was right, he'd hit Jackie up for a chance to help her instruct her class.

Jackie rounded the corner of the doorway and halted. Hands on her hips, she stared at him. "Having another break? Isn't it time for the rye bread to hit the oven?"

"Yeah, I guess you're right," Mark said, standing up and heading for the proofing ovens. After he walked a few steps past her, he stopped and turned around, thinking *no time like the present.* "Hey, how's your class going?"

Jackie stared him down. "Good."

Mark continued. "I wanted to offer to give you a hand. It must be difficult with so many people."

"It's not too hard. Adults tend to follow directions well."

"Still, a second pair of eyes and hands would be helpful, don't you think?"

Crossing her arms over her chest, Jackie cocked her head to the side. "What's in it for you?"

Mark spread his arms out at his sides. "Nothing. I'm just offering to help. I'm free those nights, so I could be of assistance. How many more classes are there?"

"Six." Jackie's eyes nearly bore a hole in him. "You're up to something, but I can't imagine what."

"Seriously, I only want to help the students. Give it a rest, Jack. Not everything is about you." *Dammit, pissing her off wasn't going to help.*

"I'll think about it," she said.

"Great. Let me know," he said before turning back toward the proofing ovens.

***

Watching him go, Jackie had the distinct im-pression that he wouldn't be doing it for her benefit or that of the students. She knew Mark Zutka well enough to know he only ever did something to please or benefit himself. But in this instance, she couldn't figure out the motive. Or the harm. It would definitely be easier with another set of experienced hands to help her. But Mark? There was a time when she'd really enjoyed working with him. She'd give him time to sweat it out before she said yes.

CHAPTER SEVEN

The uneven granite rocks pitched her feet in different directions. If it weren't for her sturdy hiking boots, she would have seriously hurt her ankles or worse, fallen down among the rocks. Jackie repositioned her feet; her arms outstretched like a tight rope walker. Once stabilized, she took in the view before her.

Down in the valley twisted a ribbon of blue-gray water. A covered bridge spanned the river at its narrowest, connecting an asphalt-covered road into a small enclave of faded red barns. Farther down the road, over the peaks of a stand of evergreen trees, she could see the white thrust of a church steeple in the town of Pearson. Rolling meadows surrounded the stand of trees, in which sheep grazed silently on pasture grass.

Jackie closed her eyes as a ray of sunlight struck her face. A smile broke across her delicate features, and a gentle sigh joined the chorus of birds. This was beautiful and exactly what she needed. She had forgotten how therapeutic a good hike in Groton State Forest could be on a beautiful Memorial Day weekend. *Remember to thank Jamaica again for closing the bakery and giving us this Sunday and Monday of the holiday weekend off.*

It had been a long time since she had been here. This place stuck out in her mind as the last place her father had taken the family for a day trip. She had loved hiking in the forest, exploring every new thing she found on the ground so often her mother had grabbed her hand and dragged her along. Her pleas to stop and look at amazing things were ignored. A few days later, Everett Thorndike left for work and never came home.

Her hope was to make it into town for a sandwich at the new café called Toasted but getting lost on the trail had eaten up too much of her time. Then she tried to make it up to Spruce Peak. This was her first time taking this particular hiking trail. With no cell service, the trails app on her phone was useless. *If only I hadn't lost the brochure with the trails map. Leave it to me to choose the wrong path where it diverged.* Tucking her arms through her day pack, she shoved the pack onto her back. It was getting on in the evening, and she still had miles to hike back to her car.

As she turned back toward the trail, she stopped short to turn around.

"Watch out!" a man on a mountain bike yelled out as he sped past her with inches to spare.

Jackie cursed aloud as she stumbled backward and fell hard on her ass. A cloud of colorful words erupted from her lips as she sat on the ground.

The biker cast a glance over his shoulder. Seeing the harm he had caused, he skidded to a halt, gravel flying, turned his bike around, and rode back to where Jackie sat. Dismounting, he offered his hand to help her up, his helmet giving his outfit a sinister look. "Here you go," he said. "Sorry about that. Not used to seeing hikers on this trail."

Glaring at him, Jackie ignored his hand. Even with the helmet, there was no mistaking him. "What are you doing here?"

Mark dropped his proffered hand and took off his helmet. "What do you mean, what am I doing here? What does it look like I'm doing?"

"Mowing down hikers on peaceful trails?"

Mark shook his head. "No, just you, Thorndike."

"Is mountain biking even allowed on red-blazed trails?" Jackie asked as she got up, again ignoring Mark's offered hand.

"Reds are multi-use. Blue-blazed trails are hiking only."

Jackie wiped the dirt from her pants. "Great. I guess I better watch out for more lunatics like you on my way back to my car."

"Where'd you leave it?" he asked, tapping his helmet tucked under his arm.

"At the parking lot off Route 131. Why?"

Mark shook his head. "That's a long way from here. It'll be dark before you get back there," he said. "Did you bring a headlamp or flashlight?"

Jackie felt the heat rising in her chest. Of course she didn't bring any lighting gear. She hadn't thought to bring anything like that. Then, she hadn't expected to get lost for so long either. "No, I didn't intend to be out here so long." Jackie shook her head.

Mark muttered under his breath, "Rookie mistake."

"What was that?" Jackie snapped, hands on her hips, her right hip cocked out.

"Never mind." Mark dropped his head back. "You can't be walking out in the woods this time of year without the appropriate equipment," he said, setting down his helmet. He shrugged off a small backpack and zipped it open. He rummaged for a few seconds before extracting a headlamp. "Here, take this. You're going to need it more than I will."

Staring at his offering, Jackie didn't flinch. "What makes you think I can't make it back in time?"

"Look, Thorndike," he said, looking at his watch. "It's seven o'clock now. Sunset is at around eight. Exactly how long did it take you to get this far from your car?" Mark frowned at her.

Jackie knew she was going to be in trouble. It had taken her nearly four hours to get this far after that wrong turn. If she left now, she'd still be walking the trail in darkness before arriving at her car. "Won't you need it?" she asked.

"I'll be back to my car in two hours. Besides, you'll be walking in the forest, which is even darker than out on the open bike trail," he added. "Take the damn headlamp."

Unable to refute what he said, Jackie snatched the light from his hand. She muttered, "thanks" before putting it over her shoulder.

"That's not where —"

"I know where it goes. But it's not dark yet so can it Zutka."

She turned away and started heading back for the trail. Something in her gut told her to check the lamp. Pulling it off her shoulder, she hit the switch, all while Mark looked on. Nothing. "Really sweet of you to lend me your headlamp, but the batteries are dead." She threw it at him.

"Let me have a look." Mark snatched it up and fumbled with it. "So much for that idea." He threw the lamp back into his backpack, feeling disgusted with himself. "Whelp, there's only one solution. You'll have to ride with me."

Jackie spun around to glare at him. "That's not a tandem bike. How the hell are we going to do that?"

"Very carefully," Mark muttered again, righting the mountain bike and climbing on. "I'll straddle the bar, like so." He stood far forward of the seat. "You sit on the seat and hang on."

Fists planted on her hips; Jackie shook her head. "Are you nuts?"

"Got a better plan, princess?" Mark ground through clenched teeth. All ready his crotch was aching from hitting the bar one too many times.

She stared at him, still shaking her head. Then she shrugged, took a step toward him and the bike. "How do I even get on this thing?"

As he steadied the bike with one hand, Mark held out the other to her. She grasped it and his shoulder with her free hand. Flinging her leg over the seat, she scooched up onto it while Mark struggled to keep the bike upright.

"Stop wiggling!" He grunted, one hand trying to hold on to the handlebars.

"I'm trying to get situated."

Mark grumbled and let go of her hand.

"I need that to hold onto."

"Tough. I'll need it to steer. Find something else to hang on to."

Behind him he felt her fumbling around, obviously not wanting to hold on to him. He steeled himself for her touch. It didn't come but they couldn't wait much longer. "Here we go," Mark called over his shoulder, pressing his foot down on the pedal. The bike lurched forward, jerking Jackie backward. Her arms flailed as her butt started to slide off the seat. Then her hands reached out for the only thing available—Mark's waist.

The bike shuddered, gathering speed as Mark pumped the pedals. Sweat beaded on his forehead despite the descending evening chill on the mountainside. They traveled for nearly a half-mile, the bike skidding and lurching along under the strain of two bodies. Shadows deepened as they wheeled along the uneven dirt trail. Most of the route along the tree line, brighter than in the forest, but with the sun setting behind them, the darkness grew across their path faster than Mark had expected.

Suddenly, the bike slid sideways over a patch of loose gravel. Both Mark and Jackie tumbled off, landing in a heap together, chest to chest and nose to nose, Jackie on top of Mark.

"Are you hurt?" Mark asked, holding on to her, his arms holding her steady.

Jackie met his gaze. She heaved a big groan. "Ugh, um, no. I don't think so."

"Don't get up too fast. Just rest a minute."

They lay together for a few seconds, catching their breath. Mark becoming aware of the contours of her body with each added second. Her lips were inches away and the desire to crush his lips to hers for the first time in eight years took his breath away. Like a drowning man, he wanted to cling to her, for air, for life.

Jackie's eyes clouded over. Did she sense his need? His desires? He could feel his body responding. Pressed directly against him, Jackie had to be feeling it too.

She rolled off him abruptly and stood up.

Mark closed his eyes and willed his body to stand down. Back in control, he got up. "Aw, shit."

"What?" She looked over at him, brushing dirt from her clothes. "What's wrong?"

He walked over to the bike, picked it up off the ground, and pointed to the front wheel. "It's broken."

"No!" Jackie walked over to examine the front tire, now bent at a forty-five-degree angle. "Can you fix it?"

"Not a chance." Mark flung the bike down on the ground.

Jackie crossed her arms over her chest, her forehead creased, eyebrows pinched together. "Wonderful." Sarcasm and frustration filled her voice. "I don't suppose you've got a spare?"

Mark shook his head and rubbed the nape of his neck. "We're still miles from the parking lot. We can't walk in the dark. It's too dangerous." He looked around, up into the forest on the hill above the trail. "We'll have to spend the night out here."

"Sleep out here? Together? Alone?" Her voice pitched up an octave and cracked.

"What other option is there? There's no cell service for miles. I don't have any flares or emergency beacons."

"Rookie mistake." Jackie snapped.

Mark sneered, "Do you have any, princess?"

Whispering sheepishly, Jackie replied, "No. Sorry."

"Well then." He searched around, stomped up into the forest, gathering hemlock and pine boughs, piling them together.

Jackie stood watching. "Building a bonfire? You have matches?"

"No. Do you?" Mark stopped, waiting for her response.

Jackie shook her head. "What should I do?"

It was oddly satisfying seeing his boss unprepared and indecisive. "Stay out of my way." Mark snapped. "How about you find out how much water we have?" *That will keep her busy.*

He continued to stack evergreen branches into a soft pile until she came back. "We have about a quart of water between us." She reported.

He nodded. "Come over here." He took his lightweight jacket out of his backpack. "You might as well lie down. I'll spread my jacket over us both as best I can."

Closing her eyes, she dropped her head before settling down on the pile on her right side. "It's pretty lumpy."

"Sorry, your highness. Next time make a reservation in advance." Mark smirked, shaking his head as he settled down, spooning her, and spread his jacket over them both. He slung his arm over her side and immediately felt her body stiffen.

"Hey!"

"What else am I going to do with my arm? Relax. I'm trying to keep us both warm. It's going to get cold up here on the mountain tonight."

She shifted restlessly about.

"What's wrong, you got a boyfriend waiting at home?"

She stiffened. "None of your business."

He chuckled, "I'll take that as a no. We've got no heat, no light, and no food. You might as well go to sleep."

She shifted around some more as if trying to refute his statement but finding nothing, remained silent.

Mark felt the tension leave her body slowly. The light was gone minutes after they settled. Buzzing insects and woodland noises erupted as they lay quiet. In a while, when Mark was sure the soft snoring noises were from Jackie, he shut his own eyes and allowed himself to drift off to sleep, the familiar scent of her hair and feel of her body settling his nerves.

CHAPTER EIGHT

Grunting noises and heavy breathing brought Jackie to a semi-awakened state. That and the cold, damp chill that had settled over her lower limbs beyond the cover of Mark's jacket. The heavy breathing was Mark, snuggled up to her backside, his mouth inches from her left ear. Not only was he spooning her, with his left arm flung over her chest, but his hand was cupping her breast. Just like old times, Jackie mused as she gingerly brushed his arm and hand away. He grunted, smacking his lips, then settled back down, his hand on her hip. She moved away, putting more distance between them.

She lay there a few minutes, trying to fall back asleep. But she was colder now. Out from under the jacket and away from Mark's body heat, Jackie's muscles were tensing up. She started to shiver, her teeth chattering. She didn't have to look to know her nipples were rock hard from the cold. *Could I roll over and get my front side warm for a little while?*

Moving inch by inch back toward him, she maneuvered her body, turning to face Mark. He stirred. She stopped all movements. When he seemed to fall back asleep, she moved the last four inches up against him. Settled at last, Jackie closed her eyes, relishing the warmth her chest had been craving.

"Were the girls feeling cold?" Mark's gruff voice asked.

Her eyes popped open at his voice. "You're awake," She whispered.

"Why are you whispering? We're all alone. In the woods." Mark rubbed his nose. Whether it itched or was cold, Jackie wasn't sure.

"Go back to sleep." She shut her eyes again and willed him to do the same.

"I'm feeling nostalgic; I remember the last time we were together. We went camping at Isle La Motte in Lake Champlain." Now he had lowered his voice nearly to a whisper.

"Shhh."

"It was a beautiful weekend. I remember the moonlight on your bare skin was radiant when we went skinny dipping." His breath, warm and soft, tickled her ear. "You are beautiful."

She looked into his eyes, just inches away, feeling the heat radiating from him. As she watched, he bent his head, and his lips pressed softly into hers.

A warmth spread through her as her lips responded, giving back, softly, sweetly. Her tongue searched out his, touching, teasing, tasting. The warmth flared in her body, spreading like lava. Dazed and sleepy, her mind conjured up that night in the camp so long ago. Beside the glowing embers of the fading campfire. An aura of light, the scent of wood smoke hovering in the air. Mark cupping her head, holding her close for a long slow, lazy kiss that left her breathless, her heart thumping and her parts vibrating in song.

Her hands, clutching his shirt, searched underneath, skimming across his hard molded chest, feeling the taut muscles as he dipped again to the oasis of her kisses. Ripples of desire surged through her like waves on the lake beach. Soft, continuous, insistent. His hands found her breasts, his thumbs the hardened peaks. Through her clothes, he fondled them. Her breath caught in her throat with the ecstasy of the sensation, raising the aching longing down her body.

"I need you." The words were out of her mouth before she realized what she was saying. Her entire body shook, her heart skittered in her chest. She broke off the kiss and struggled to sit up. "No. Wait. I can't. We can't," She added breathlessly. She pulled back adding space between them.

Mark raised his hands away from her, letting her go. "We could. But if you don't want to, you're the boss."

"That's not what I meant, but yes that's part of the problem. We can't do this again. Not now."

He raised an eyebrow. "Maybe, maybe not. But no is no. I respect that." He rolled over onto his other side giving her his back.

The abrupt closure of the conversation wasn't what she expected. Unsettled further, she didn't know what to do or say. A part of her still wanted to say, "Screw it, I've missed you, where were we?" and the other part wanted to stay firm in her gut reaction. Reconciling herself to the end of the intimacy, she too rolled onto her other side. Back-to-back now, she closed her eyes, trying not to feel the heat of his body inches away under the shared jacket. And trying not to remember their camping trip together, that last idyllic weekend before everything hit the proverbial fan.

***

Chirping birds woke Mark. He didn't stir but his eyes opened. It wasn't dawn yet though what was visible of the eastern sky through the trees was beginning to lighten. Reaching behind him, he found he had enough room to roll onto his back. Jackie didn't move as he did. Staring up at the tree canopy, he thought about what almost happened. Gradually his memory of their last night together flooded his mind. Closing his eyes, he settled into the images he'd replayed hundreds of times over the last eight years.

Wrapping her leg around his as they lay inside the tent, she said, "I need you."

"Baby, I'll never stop needing you," Mark whispered in her ear, his hand slipping past the waistband of her pants to the apex of her thighs.

Again, Jackie's breath hitched in her throat, her voice cracking. "Yes, please." She urged when Mark slipped his fingers lower. The tremors in his groin deepened with her vocalizations.

Her hips pressed into his touch, begging far more than her lips as the want grew to need, need grew to necessity, necessity grew to demand. "Please!" Her hands rubbed the front of his jeans, stroking the length of him. The fire burning in her belly, the inferno only Mark knew how to satisfy.

"Do you want me?" Mark asked. "Here? Now?" He backed away from her, waiting for her response. His hands off her.

"Yes," Jackie breathed, taking a moment to kick off her hiking boots, shimmy out of her jeans and panties, slip off her shirt and bra.

Mark watched as she shed her clothes, only moving forward when she beckoned him to her. Aiding her as she worked to rid him of his clothes, adding them to the pile of her own.

"Wait, I need my wallet." He reached for his jeans, dragging them back.

"Why?"

He cocked his head and smiled at her. "Protection." Mark extracted the foil packet and threw the jeans aside.

A thrill ran through her as she reached out and wrapped her fingers around him. Hissing, his head flung back, and his eyes closed, he let her have her way for a few moments before stopping her hand. "Easy woman, or the show will be all over too soon."

Chuckling, she let go. Mark pressed her back onto the mattress. "Let me see if you still taste as sweet."

The warmth of his lips and the wetness of his tongue nearly kicked her over the edge. As it was, alone on the side of the mountain, she pleaded out loud for him to fill her. Her fingers sank into Mark's tousled hair as he tasted and teased her.

"Mark, I can't wait much longer. Please, darling. Please."

Mark sank back on his heels and donned the condom. Ready, he began another long slow tease, sinking inside inch by inch. Jackie moaning and sighing, urging him deeper still until he was fully seated against her.

When he withdrew, easing back, she begged again. Returning home, she felt the fullness he brought, the ache still there, still unfulfilled. Mark's thrusts were painstakingly slow and teasing, driving

Jackie into a frenzy of pleading. Her hands reaching out, her body quivering like a string, stretched taut, waiting to release, to break in two.

"Faster," she called.

"No. Slow and mind-blowing." He continued his slow dance into and out of her wetness. "Look at me."

She reached down for her mound, but he pushed her hand aside. "Not yet." He was breathing heavy now, the strain of control, of composure, of restraint nearing the end. And with the next thrust forward, he gently touched her spot. And together, their string broke.

They lay in each other's arms, naked, satisfied, warm.

On the edge of sleep now, here, on this mountain side eight years later, Mark rolled over to face Jackie's sleeping figure. "I remember every nuance of making love to you exactly how you like it. Every pleasure point, every sign and sigh and what it means." Mark whispered into her ear. "Maybe someday." He rolled onto his back, closed his eyes again letting sleep take him.

A fireball of light drilled into his eyes. Mark flung his arm over them and tried to roll over, but there was a body preventing it. He sat up. A squirrel was investigating his cycling shoe. As quietly as he could, he pitched a pine cone at it, shooing the animal away, hoping he wouldn't awaken the sleeping woman curled up beside him. As he watched the rodent scamper off, he saw his broken bike ten feet away beside the trail.

His morning stiffy calling, he tried to get up without waking her, but Jackie stirred as he stood. Moving slowly, he made as little noise as possible on his way deeper into the woods for a bio break.

While he stood behind a stand of saplings, he heard, "Oh. My. God." A frantic rustling sound filled the silence. Peeking around the leaves after tucking himself back together, he saw Jackie hastily scrambling to get up.

He smiled. So willing initially last night and so appalled at even the aborted attempt this morning. Having given her time to pull herself together, he started whistling as he returned to their makeshift lover's nest. "Good morning!" He said with all the gusto he had in his heart. Ignoring her glare, he added, "How are you this fine morning?"

"Let's get going," Jackie barked, re-lacing on her hiking boots. "We have a long walk."

"True. But isn't it a beautiful day? The sun is shining, not a cloud in the sky." He threw open his hands and stared up into the sun for effect.

"Forget it." Jackie stomped back to the trail, leaving Mark nearly doubled over with laughter.

She stopped, glaring again at him. "What's so funny?"

"You. You were singing a very different tune for a little while last night." He rubbed his chin and watched her face intently.

"Stuff it, Mark. That was a momentary loss of, well—"

"Control?" Mark smirked.

"Look, it was cold. I was cold. Things almost got out of hand."

"I'll say."

"Stop. Just Stop." She held up her palm. "Last night didn't mean anything. Doesn't change anything."

Mark rubbed the nape of his neck. "It doesn't?"

"No. You still don't believe me when I tell you I didn't steal it."

Mark advanced on her until they were toe to toe. The pent-up anger from long ago came bubbling back. His eyes burned down into hers. "You're right about that. That's not what Paul told me. And Paul and I go back a long way. Much longer than you and I. Besides, what does that have to do with our near escapade last night?"

"We can never be friends again until you believe me. Or lovers." Jackie stated, very matter-of-factly, before walking off down the trail, leaving Mark behind.

CHAPTER NINE

Six in the morning, the day after their return from the forest, and all the breads were either made and cooling or still in the oven baking. Mark watched as Jackie took off her apron and headed for the sales room, apparently intent on a cup of coffee and something to eat for breakfast. He pondered whether this was the right time to spring his offer. Co-instructing her bakery class was paramount to his plans to apply for the KMF assistant baking instructor's job.

Mark thought back to Sunday when he'd serendipitously come across Jackie while biking. Being able to help her had been a stroke of luck, especially since she needed it to get out of those woods. Or would have if his bike hadn't crashed and broken beyond repair.

His body stirred at the memory of holding her again. It had been so long since she'd left the pastry program and him in one swoop. It had ended so badly. Would their history, coupled with what transpired in the forest hurt his request? The way he saw it, she owed him a big favor now. She was in a position for a reasonable amount of arm twisting.

All the previous week, he had been careful to follow orders, watch his step and do nothing wrong at the bakery. He wanted to be on her best side in as many ways as possible to get to that "yes" answer. And he would do whatever else it took. Within reason, of course.

Jackie came shuffling back through the kitchen door, a mug of steaming coffee in one hand and what looked like an apple-cinnamon muffin in the other. She sat down at their break table as the door swung shut. After setting her breakfast down, she picked up the morning paper and began reading the front page. Every few minutes, her right hand reached out to grasp her coffee cup and bring the piping hot liquid to her lips for a sip.

Mark weighed the timing. When she put down the paper to pick up her muffin, he strode over to the table and sat down across the table from her. "How's the muffin?" he asked after she had taken her first bite.

She flashed a steely glare at him before refocusing on her newspaper. Chewing a few times before swallowing, she answered. "Great." She took another bite of the muffin before washing it down with a sip of coffee, turning her body away from him.

"I've been wanting to ask you something," he said, looking down at his hands folded together on the tabletop.

She sighed, dropping the paper to her lap. "What is it Zutka? Get it off your chest so I can read and eat in peace."

Glancing up to look her in the eyes, Mark took a breath and said, "I'd like to help you with your bakery class."

As he finished saying the sentence, Mark saw Jackie's eyes turn wary. Hastily, he added, "Fifteen is a lot of people to keep your two eyes on, and I thought I could, you know, give you a hand with the class. You would still be the instructor; I would just be there to assist as needed."

Jackie stared him down. "Why?" Her forehead wrinkled and her eyes narrowed.

Mark tried not to squirm in his seat. "Why not? I'm free those nights. I always liked the idea of showing other people how to bake. I love what I do. Why not share it?"

"I don't think it's such a good idea." Glancing away, she bit into her muffin again and chewed thoughtfully.

"Why is that?"

"Because there's one thing I learned during culinary school. Mark Zutka doesn't do things unless they have some significance to him. There's got to be something you're not telling me."

"Maybe that's the way I was in school, but things are different now. I'm different now. I only want to help you. And, as I said, I would enjoy it." Mark sat back in the chair, trying hard not to strangle a yes out of Jackie's throat. "Besides, didn't I give you my headlamp when you were out hiking? I had no ulterior motive for that other than to see that you got to your car safely."

"A headlamp with dead batteries."

"But I got us both safely out of the forest, didn't I?"

"Let's not go into that fiasco." Gulping her coffee, Jackie picked up her paper, fighting with it to get the page open correctly.

Mark sat forward a little in the chair, leaning on his arms crossed on the table top. "Look, why not give it a try one night. You can always change your mind and tell me to go pound flour."

Jackie popped the last piece of muffin into her mouth and chewed slowly. She sat staring at Mark as if willing him to blink. He tried desperately not to make any movement that would deter her from complying.

After a minute, Jackie blinked. "Okay. One class. This week. Puff Pastry. Get there half an hour early to help me set up."

Mark tried not to breathe a sigh of relief. "Great," he said. "I'll see you there." He got up from the table just as an oven alarm went off. As he headed for the oven to remove the freshly baked loaves of oatmeal and quinoa bread, Jackie called him back.

"Don't think this has anything to do with what transpired that night. Because it doesn't." Jackie said, her gaze narrowed and defiant before she stalked away.

Over his shoulder, he caught sight of Jackie disappearing into the locker room. Only then did he pump his fist in victory.

She returned a few minutes later and handed him a sheet of paper. "Here's the lesson plan for tonight."

Mark sat down at the break table as he took the sheet from her. "Ribbons, tarts, stars, Palmiers, and cones?" he said as he perused the list.

"Yes, and if there's time, stuffed puff pastry pretzels. But I'm thinking we won't get that far."

"What do you want me to do?" Mark asked.

"Flip the sheet over."

He did as instructed.

"Here's a list of the prep work we have to do before the students get there."

"Why don't you have the students do this work?" Mark asked, frowning at the list.

Jackie glared at him. "Because there is only so much time, and I'd rather we spent it doing puff pastry designs rather than measuring and mixing ingredients. They know how to do that already."

Mark's eyes roamed the list. He remained silent.

"Come by at six instead, unless you've changed your mind about helping."

Mark cocked his head with a smug smile. "I'll be there."

"Okay, before class you need to make the pastry creme and the cheese mixtures for the ribbons. I'll make the palmier filling and prep the fruit for the tarts."

"What about during class? What do you want me to do?" Mark asked, dropping the sheet on the table top.

"I'll take care of the front two rows of students. You take care of the back rows of students."

"Why do I get three rows, and you only get two?" he inquired, his head cocked to the side again.

"Because I will also be doing all the verbal instruction." She turned on him, hands on her hips and her petite frame rigid. "Look, I didn't ask you to help me. You asked to be a part of this. Either we do things my way, or you're out." Folding her arms over her chest, she glowered at him.

Mark sighed and nodded.

"As I was saying, you get to watch and do one-on-ones with the students," Jackie explained. "I can't give instruction and watch more students. Not in this lesson."

"Fine." He crumpled up the paper and shoved it deep into his pants pocket before walking away in the direction of the sounding oven timer. "I'll be there. Early."

That evening, Mark arrived at the high school cooking classroom exactly at six o'clock as Jackie had requested. Still, she was already there when he arrived, slicing strawberries.

"Everything you need for the pastry creme is on the counter beside the stove," she said, not waiting for him to remove his jacket.

Mark donned the apron he'd brought and set to work measuring the milk and sugar together and setting them to boil on the stove. In a separate bowl, he cracked open the eggs and measured in cornstarch and more sugar. After combining the two mixtures when the milk was boiling, he set the pan aside to cool and added the vanilla.

Satisfied with the creme, he walked over to get the cheese mixture ingredients and recipe from Jackie. She had finished prepping the fruit and was mixing together cinnamon and sugar for the palmier filling.

"Where's the cheese topping recipe and the ingredients?" he asked, standing on the opposite side of the workbench in front of Jackie.

"They're in the last brown grocery bag on the counter," she said, gesturing toward a line of five bags.

"Which is the first bag, and which is the last?" Mark asked.

Jackie sighed and set down her wooden spoon. She walked over to the bags, picked up the one on the right, and held it out for him.

"Thanks," Mark said, shaking his head. "You could have just told me the one on the far right."

Jackie glared at him. "Just zip it. Don't make me think it's a mistake for you to help me. Already."

Taking the bag, Mark went to the back counter of the room seething. *Women and their hormonal upsets. Geesh.*

He made the recipe in the bowl he also found in the bag, finishing just as the students started to arrive.

Stepping aside, he stayed at the back of the room to let Jackie handle them. After everyone was present, she started. "Tonight, Chef Mark Zutka is assisting me. There's so many of you, and this is a very hands-on class tonight." As the students turned around to get a look at him, Mark waved hello and smiled.

Jackie started the class with the tarts. "Cut the pastry into squares. Brush along a one-half inch of the edges with your egg wash. Fold the edges over toward the center of the dough, keeping it square." Jackie demonstrated in the air with a piece of square paper.

He marveled at how she interacted with the students; answering questions, patiently explaining again and offering encouragement. If he was going to get the job at KMF, he would have to learn to do the same.

Mark shuddered as he watched an elderly man fold the pastry backward instead of forward toward the center. He stepped up to the man's side. "No, sir, the other way."

"Huh," the man said, suddenly dropping the pastry dough on the bench top.

Picking it up, Mark unfolded the side the man had folded wrong and gestured for him to watch. "Here—it goes like this." He demonstrated the correct folding pattern.

"Ah," the man said as Mark set the pastry down in front of him and watched silently as the man continued to do it wrong. Grinding his teeth as he watched, he counted to twenty before stepping in again and showing the man the right way to do it. That time the man got it correct.

Stepping aside, Mark surveyed the rest of his students. No one else was having a problem with the tart, and they finished and moved on to the cheese ribbon once their baking sheets were in the ovens.

No one had a problem doing the zigzag formation and skewering of the dough. Once the tarts came out of the oven, the baking sheet of cheese ribbons went in next.

The class went on to Palmiers, or elephant ears as they were sometimes called. Everyone seemed to get the folding done correctly but needed help setting them on the baking sheet in the correct V-pattern.

When each person's ribbons came out of the ovens, the Palmiers went in to bake.

Jackie took a breath. Next up, the class was working on stars. "Cut a square of pastry dough." When everyone had done so, she continued. "Now, cut a diagonal line from the tip of the corner to within three-quarters of an inch of the center of the pastry." Jackie waited as everyone did as told. "Now, the tricky part—fold over every other corner to the center of the pastry and press to seal at the center." She held up a square of paper already cut correctly and demonstrated the folding over process.

Both Mark and Jackie had to help several people get the folding instruction right.

Mark felt good after doing so, though the elderly man had been difficult and tried his patience.

Lastly, the class started the cones. They began by wrapping sugar ice-cream cones with aluminum foil. Although Mark had thought this design would be difficult for them, all but the elderly man got the instructions perfectly. Mark helped the man, standing side by side with him, doing one cone while the man did another.

The last of the cones came out of the oven as the students were finishing decorating the tarts with a layer of pastry creme and an array of sliced fruits.

By eight-forty, everyone began packing away their creations in containers they had brought. There was a lot of laughter as they tasted and compared the pastries.

When the last student left, Jackie came over to Mark. Her eyes softened, and she held out her hand to shake. "Thanks for being here tonight. As much as I hate to admit it, there's no way I could have gotten through this class without you."

Mark shook her hand. "My pleasure—though Mr. Kimble gave me a run on my patience."

"Yeah, he's a real sweetheart, but definitely a novice in the kitchen. His heart is in the right place, and he really wants to learn."

Jackie glanced at her watch. "Oh, we have ten minutes to get out of here."

They scurried to straighten out the classroom and pack up and were the last instructors out of the building before lockup.

Mark helped carry the supplies out to the parking lot where their two cars were the only remaining vehicles. It was on the tip of his tongue to ask her if she wanted to get a beer with him. But before he could get the words out, she'd climbed behind the wheel, nodded briskly, and driven away.

CHAPTER TEN

Sitting at the kitchen table, Jackie sipped her coffee, her head hidden behind the comics page from Sunday's paper. It was blissfully quiet for a change, except for the ambient hum of the air handling system. And a kneading machine working on another batch of wheat bread dough. She looked up. It was way too quiet. Turning around to look, not a single baker was in sight.

Where did everyone go?

Curiosity got the better of her. She checked the locker room and bathroom. Both rooms were empty. So was the pantry, storage room, and walk-in refrigerator. Her interest escalated. There was only one other place they could all be: in the sales room.

As she approached the kitchen door, it swung open. Holding a decorated cake with a flickering candle in the middle, Mark appeared in the doorway. Isabelle, Jenny, and Vanessa peeked out from behind him, yelling, "Happy birthday!" Everyone broke into a chorus of the birthday song.

She stood there, surrounded by the people she worked with, her face flushed, her eyes glowing, and a hand over her heart. When they finished singing, she hugged all of them except Mark. "Thank you! Who told you it was my birthday?"

"Mark did." Came an echo of voices.

She turned to him, a queer warm and fuzzy feeling in the center of her chest. Her eyes filled with tears. "Mark." He had remembered her birthday when her own mother hadn't even called or sent a card.

"Never mind. Make a wish and blow out the damn candles before the smoke detector and sprinkler system go off."

She did as she was told. A couple of cheers sounded along with words like, "Great." And "I'm hungry." And "Somebody get a knife and plates."

Looking at the cake, Jackie chuckled. "I recognize this one. Looks like the one I made yesterday."

"Yup, you did. You made your own birthday cake."

Laughing out loud at that, she added, "I thought it was odd the order said 'no writing'. I guess Isabelle added it later."

A few of them disappeared to wait on customers while the rest of them ate slices of Italian fruit cake: two layers of yellow sponge cake separated by fresh-cut peaches and strawberries mixed into whipped cream.

"Thanks, Mark." She placed her hand on his forearm and gave it a squeeze.

His head nodded. "Happy birthday, Jackie." With a flourish, he brought out a gift bag from behind a cardboard box.

The remaining crew gathered closer as she reached into the brightly colored gift bag and pulled out a headlamp. Jackie started to laugh, while Mark looked on amused. She pressed the button, and the light came on. She laughed even harder, her eyes twinkling as she looked at Mark.

"A headlamp?" Isabelle asked, her face lit with surprise and curiosity.

"Private joke," Jackie said, feeling the rush of blood staining her cheeks as she remembered their night together on the mountain.

Realizing they weren't going to get any better explanation, the crowd dispersed, leaving Mark and Jackie alone.

"You shouldn't have." Jackie gestured with the headlamp.

Mark cocked his head. "I might not always be around to keep you out of trouble."

"Thank you." She brushed a kiss on his cheek and disappeared into the locker room.

After work that day, Jackie arrived home to find the mail had been delivered, as usual. As she had been doing for the last two weeks, she swiftly flipped through all the envelopes, looking, hoping, to see one with a Harwich, Vermont return address.

Today, there it was. A crisp, white business envelope addressed to her with a King Mills Flour return address. Jackie dropped the remaining mail and tore into the envelope immediately.

Dear Ms. Thorndike,

Thank you for your recent application for the job opening of assistant baking instructor at King Mills Flour. We have reviewed your credentials and would be pleased to meet with you for an interview to discuss your suitability for the job.

Please contact Mrs. Chester at 555-4758 to set up an appointment with me at your convenience.

Sincerely,

Frank Goss

Director, King Mills Flour Baking School

The breath she had been holding since opening the envelope came out in a whoosh. *They reviewed my credentials and they're still going to give me an interview.* Jackie remembered how she had listed her time with the Baking and Pastry Arts Program. The application had only asked for dates of attendance. It had not asked if she had graduated though she would have thought they would check for that accomplishment.

Jackie looked at her watch. It was late afternoon but still worth a try. She dialed the number given and heard it ring several times before a woman answered.

"King Mills Flour Company Baking School Instruction Office," the woman said.

"I'd like to speak with Mrs. Chester, please," Jackie said, quickly referring to the letter for the correct name.

"This is she. How can I help you?"

"I received a letter requesting I call to set up an appointment for an interview with Frank Goss."

"Yes, who may I ask is calling?" the woman asked.

"This is Jackie Thorndike." Jackie fiddled with the paper before setting it down. She began searching for a pen so she could write down the appointment particulars.

"Yes, Ms. Thorndike, would next Wednesday, June 5th at 2 pm work for you?"

Jackie turned to look at her calendar. Wednesday was free, but wow, so fast. She felt lightheaded at the speed with which this was coming at her. Finally, she answered Mrs. Chester. "Yes, that would be fine. Thank you."

"Wonderful. When you arrive, please come to the Baking School Instruction Office, which is all the way down the main hallway on your right."

"Yes, thank you. Should I bring anything?" Jackie scribbled the instructions down on the back of the letter along with the appointment date and time.

"No but do come prepared to give a ten-minute lecture on any topic you wish."

Jackie stood stunned, her mouth agape. It stood to reason that they would want to see her in action, but Jackie was still surprised. "All right, thank you," Jackie said. "See you then," she added before disconnecting the call.

Hugging the phone to her chest, she grinned. "Happy birthday to me!"

***

Staring at the same spot on the wall for over half an hour hadn't helped. She still didn't have any idea what she would give as her presentation. Every topic she thought of seemed either too complicated or too easy. She needed something that could show off her baking knowledge and her ability to connect with the audience on their level. Flipping through her previous lesson plans had given her a few ideas, but some of them were contingent on having props, and she didn't know if they would be available.

Sighing, she closed her eyes and pitched forward, resting her forehead on the table.

"Are you alright?" Mark's deep voice asked as she heard his footsteps enter the kitchen.

She didn't move. "Yes, I'm just thinking." She heard Mark's footfalls head for the locker room; heard the creak as the door opened and then swung shut.

Sighing again, she thanked God that Mark hadn't asked any more questions.

Hot breath streamed along the back of her neck. Jackie jolted upright, and her eyes flew open to find Mark behind her. He broke into a sinister laugh as he walked away, watching her over his shoulder.

"I thought you were in the locker room," Jackie exclaimed, her hand clasped to the back of her neck.

Mark grinned wildly. "Fooled ya."

"Did you have to do that?" Jackie's eyes narrowing as she witnessed Mark's obvious pleasure in making her uncomfortable.

"You used to love it when I did that." He winked.

"That's before you threw me to the wolves."

"What did you expect? You lied to cover your scheme."

"I did not lie. I did not deceive you." She hissed out, not wanting the others to hear them.

"Oh, you want to talk about deceiving, do you. Let's talk about that final project in baking school if you want to talk about deceit." Mark's smile disappeared, replaced with a frown.

"Let's not," Jackie replied as she started to get up from the table.

"No." Mark wouldn't let go. "Let's talk about that day. When I found out you stole sourdough starter from my jar to replace your own. That little incident nearly got me thrown out of the culinary institute too."

"That was over eight years ago. Let it go, Mark."

"Not until I get an apology from you," he said, staring her down.

"You're not going to get an apology. I didn't steal that starter. Paul gave it to me. He told me it was discard from his starter. He swore he wouldn't tell anyone, and then he told everyone." She stood up so abruptly the chair went flying backward, hitting the floor with a thud. "What was I supposed to do? It was our final bread-baking project. Create a sourdough starter from natural airborne yeast. Nurture it for four weeks and then bake a sourdough bread on the appointed day."

Walking away from him, she turned at the industrial mixer. "But mine got contaminated. There were pink streaks in it and it smelled rotten." She shrugged. "It was just days before baking day, and I had to throw it out."

"So, you stole some of mine." Mark hitched out his hip and planted his hand on it.

Shaking her head violently, she walked back to stand before him. "No, I didn't. It was given to me. Paul gave it to me. Why can't you understand and accept that? Why can't you believe me?" Tears welled in her eyes at the memory. She turned away, the back of her hand wiping away the stray tears flowing down her cheeks.

"But he gave you half of mine."

She whirled back to him and stepped toe to toe. "I didn't know it was yours!"

Mark stared down into her eyes. "Paul told me he saw you take it from my jar."

"Paul lied. He gave me that jar. I didn't realize it was yours."

"Why would Paul do that? What would be his motive?"

Her palm swept across her forehead, "How would I know?"

"You didn't say a word to anyone. You tried to pass off the sourdough starter as your own. And you would have succeeded if not for Paul."

Jackie got to within six inches of Mark's nose. "You're right; I didn't say a word. That was my intent. I wanted to have something to use to bake my final project."

"And little Miss Perfect Thorn got caught."

"You weren't exactly the model student."

Mark frowned and glanced away.

"You were an arrogant, stubborn, inflexible, and unreliable student. How you managed to get them to give you a second chance is beyond my comprehension."

Mark stammered, "Ah, at least I was truthful. And I didn't have to be the center of attention all the time."

"Center of attention! People—" Jackie started to say, each word squeezing out between her teeth.

The proofing oven alarm went off, calling Mark to move the bread dough into the baking ovens. He stepped up to her, nearly nose to nose, his eyebrows pinched together. "The sad part is, if you had told me what happened, if you had asked, I would have gladly given you some of my sourdough."

He turned on his heel, stalking off, leaving a red-faced Jackie, flummoxed and fuming.

She didn't know what was worse. The fact that he hadn't believed her then or the fact that the incident was still dogging her.

CHAPTER ELEVEN

Jackie sprinted for the locker room when she saw the caller ID on her cell phone, ignoring Mark's questioning and astonished look as she raced by him.

"Hello? Mom? Are you okay?" She answered, popping on speakerphone as she barged through the door searching for privacy. Her pulse pounded with the exertion and the thought something must be seriously wrong. Her mom never called her unless there was some dire news.

"Jackie? You haven't called in months," boomed Alwina Thorndike's cigarette-induced hoarse voice.

"Is that it?" She closed her eyes and huffed a huge sigh. No emergency. Jackie sank down on a chair. "I've been busy training someone new. And teaching my baking class."

"Teaching a class? They let you teach baking? I thought they threw you out of that baking program because you were a rotten baker."

Jackie's breath caught in her throat. *No matter how many times I explain what happened, she still thinks they threw me out because I couldn't bake.* Scrubbing her face with her hand, she started to protest. "I —oh, never mind." She slumped back in the chair. "What are you calling for?"

"To see if you've come to your senses yet. Isn't it enough that you've been fired from two jobs? Why do you continue with this baking fancy?"

Her blood pressure skyrocketed. She jumped to her feet and to her defense. "First of all, I was not fired from Berkshire Bread. I had a one-year internship and left when my time was up. And I wasn't fired from Chang Bakery. I worked there for six years and left there to work here at Jam Bakery." She paced the floor to the back of the room.

"All I'm saying is it's time you found a real purpose."

"What do you mean?"

"Find a man." Her mother said the words with as much reverence as she might say find a prince.

"Why would I want to do that?"

"Look baby; you're almost thirty. It's time you found a man, got married, and had a family. Quit this baking bullshit. Your sister did, and she's perfectly happy."

At the mention of her sister, Camilla, her jaw tensed. "My sister has made government assistance her career. Is that really what you want for me? Public assistance, four kids, and a runaway husband?"

"Well, no. How was she to know Kenneth would leave her?" Alwina muttered.

"His character was pretty plain to me when he showed up half an hour late and drunk for their wedding." Jackie spat as she dropped down onto the chair again.

"Think about it. That's all I'm asking. Besides, I could move in and help take care of your babies."

A shudder went through her, and she breathed a heavy sigh. There's the nugget. Her mother wanted to be taken care of financially. That was the true purpose of her phone call and suggestion. Sitting up straight, Jackie squared her shoulders. There was no way she was ever going to live under the same roof with her mother ever again. "There's no need for me to think about it. I'm not the marrying type. From what I've seen, marriage and misery are one and the same."

"Honey, that's not true."

"It's not? Then explain to me where Dad has been for the last twenty years. I'll tell you; he walked out. Leaving us with no money and a mortgage. Now the house is gone to foreclosure. And you and Camilla are on welfare. Don't make marriage out to be a happy ending because it's not. That's not what I see from where I'm standing."

"Look who's feeling all hoity-toity."

Tears gushing down her cheeks, Jackie stared at the phone in her hand. She hadn't even mentioned her birthday. "You know, when the phone rang, and I saw it was you I was worried something terrible had happened to you. And then I had the thought maybe you were calling to wish me a belated happy birthday. Instead, you berate my skills, my education and my career."

"So I forgot your birthday. Haven't you gotten over the need for attention at your age?" Her mother scoffed.

"I send you a card every year. And I call."

"As well you should. You know what the Bible says: Honor thy mother and father." Her sanctimonious tone came through the phone speaker loud and clear. On a roll, she continued. "Now look. Don't be changing the subject on me. Do you really think you can make something of yourself baking cookies? Smarten up, Jackie. You're no better now than you were as a kid, trying to cook and bake like you were some famous chef on TV. You weren't a baker then, and you aren't now. You never will be."

Stunned by the attack, Jackie disconnected the call and threw the phone across the room. After all these years, her own mother still didn't believe in her. Her tears turned into sobbing. Sobbing so hard she retched into the nearest wastebasket, wounded to her core.

Large, gentle hands held her as she emptied her stomach then gathered her trembling, wailing figure to his hard chest. The warmth of his body and the smell of his favorite soap gave her ravaged spirit a small measure of comfort.

***

Mark couldn't believe what he'd overheard. When he'd seen Jackie race through the kitchen in the direction of the bathroom, he thought she was sick. But she'd veered into the locker room. *She's not the sick one. That woman who calls herself her mother is.* Years ago, she'd mentioned her mother, but he'd never met her. He fervently hoped he'd never meet up with the woman because he was already fisting his hands for her face. The things she'd said to Jackie, her daughter, were unspeakable.

His hand cupped her head, holding it close. Her wet cheek pressed to his heart; his shirt soaked through from her tears. Gently, he rocked her in his arms; his lips pressed to the top of her head, he murmured softly. "You're a wonderful baker. And a good cook."

Her sobbing trailed to quiet weeping as if she were listening to his words. Eventually, she pulled back and looked up into his eyes. Her face, ravaged by grief, was blotchy, her eyelids nearly swollen shut and crimson red.

He pressed a kiss to her forehead. "Don't believe a word she said. You're a great baker, a great pastry chef. Anyone who's seen you work can see that. A diploma from a fancy expensive culinary school program is irrelevant. Anyone can learn the skills. But you— you have the talent and instincts of a pastry chef."

Her eyes searched his as she sniffled. "You really think so?"

"Know so. Hundred percent." He nodded and tucked a strand of hair behind her ear.

She sighed and leaned into him again. "Thanks for that."

He wrapped his arms around her shoulders and gave her a squeeze. Loosening his grip, he let her rest there, enjoying the feeling of her in his arms again. He had always loved just holding her close like this. Feeling her heart beating in rhythm with his own through this chest. It had been eight years too long. Much as he hated to admit it, he'd missed her.

She didn't stay long enough for his liking. When she pulled away, putting distance between them, he grasped her hand one last time and squeezed before she escaped out the door.

CHAPTER TWELVE

Holding the sheet of paper up to the light, Jackie skimmed the words once more and tried to ingrain the instructions. Unsure if she would have to give her lesson from memory or read from notes, she decided to memorize the steps of the cranberry clafoutis.

"Step one, heat the oven to four hundred degrees Fahrenheit. Step two, pour one-quarter cup of melted butter into a nine by thirteen baking dish and use it to coat the bottom and side of the dish. Step three, whisk four eggs in a bowl until blended. Step four, in a separate bowl, whisk together one-quarter cup of sugar, one-third cup of flour, and one-half teaspoon of salt. Step five, whisk the sugar/flour mixture into the eggs. Step six, whisk one cup of milk and one-half teaspoon of vanilla into the egg mixture. Pour the batter into the prepared dish. Step seven, gently pour one cup of fresh cranberries into the batter. Step eight, bake forty to forty-five minutes until golden brown and puffy. Let cool about thirty minutes before serving."

Breathless, she sat, set down the paper, closed her eyes, and began reciting the steps from memory. Once again, she got as far as step six and forgot the vanilla. Growling at herself, she started over, eyes still closed.

Jackie heard a rustling beside her and opened her eyes to find Mark reading her lesson. "Hey, that's mine," she said, snatching it from out of his hands.

"Making a clafoutis?" Mark asked quizzically. "Cranberry instead of the traditional blueberry?"

"Yeah. Thinking about it," Jackie replied. "Tart cranberries contrast nicely with the sweet flan. It's one of my favorite desserts."

"Since when?"

Jackie crossed her arms over her chest. "Since my trip to France."

"Interesting."

"What's so interesting about that?"

"I didn't know you had ever been to France," Mark replied.

"That's where I fell in love with pastry and decided I wanted to be a pastry chef."

"And yet, here you are, working full time as a bread baker. Interesting."

"Until Jamaica left on maternity leave, yes. Someday, I hope Jamaica will need another permanent pair of hands in pastry making, and I can move right into that job."

"So, you've spent the last seven years working as a bread baker everywhere you've gone when all you've really wanted to do was pastry."

"My job in Boston allowed me to help with the pastries, though bread baking was the crux of my job."

Mark's eyes widened. "Right, Isabelle was telling me you came here from Chang's. Great place. Why did you leave?"

Jackie didn't want to have to explain herself to Mark. Especially to Mark. And she didn't want to let it slip that she was applying to teach baking skills at King Mills. That information was on a need-to-know basis, and he was definitely not needing to know.

She looked past Mark to the clock on the wall. It was quitting time. "Well, I'd love to chit-chat with you, but it's time to leave." Turning, she headed for the locker room, her lesson instructions securely grasped in her hand.

"Wait. I have something for you. It's in the locker room." He followed on her heels, then dug into his locker, removing his backpack. From inside it he withdrew a large manila envelope.

"What's this?" Jackie asked when he held it out to her.

"It's the market analysis for the sprouted bread idea I had."

Jackie's eyes were wary as she took the envelope. She stuffed it in her own locker, grabbed her purse and slammed the door shut.

***

"Aren't you going to look at it?" Mark called after her as she headed out the locker room door.

"Tomorrow." She threw the words over her shoulder, adding, "Don't forget class tonight."

Mark watched her go, forgetting the envelope and smiled. *Clafoutis.* He followed her. "What's on the lesson plan tonight for baking class?"

"Clafoutis and quiche," Jackie called out on the way out the bakery's back door.

"I thought it was supposed to be pâte à choux?"

Jackie turned back. "It was. But I changed the plan. It's clafoutis and quiche instead."

"Great." Mark knew that hadn't been the original plan. He mulled over the change in his brain. Jackie was going to try out her teaching skill on the French custard tonight as a practice run for her interview teaching session. That had to be her motive for suddenly changing out tonight's scheduled class on baking creme puffs and eclairs. This was good. He'd also get a chance to see if her method of instruction succeeded. Perhaps he'd even copy it if it were good. Or maybe he'd do the quiche instruction for his interview. Mark shuffled back to the locker room to change into street attire, all the while thinking of tonight's lesson plan and which instruction would sound more favorable for his own interview teaching session.

Later that evening, Mark took the ladder steps gingerly, as quietly as he could so as not to alert his brother to his movement. Even so, a creak of the wood plank at the bottom of the loft ladder was all it took. He cringed as he heard the creak and the resulting response from the kitchen area.

"Hey, before you go!" Joe called from the kitchen as Mark walked swiftly toward the cabin door.

Mark came to a halt, his hand on the front door latch. "What? Hurry up or I'm going to be late for class." He needed to get to the high school before Jackie did. It was the principle of the thing. He needed to prove to her he could be relied on.

"I have another hot date this Saturday." Joe walked over and poked Mark in the chest with each word. "I need you to stay out."

"Okay." Mark said, as he opened the door.

Joe grabbed the door and held it. "I mean it, bro. No screwups this time or you're out on your ass instantly and forever more. Understood?"

Mark and Joe's eyes connected and held. Joe's steely gaze bore into his. There was still a lot of resentment between them about the last episode. Michelle had never forgiven Joe or Mark for the coitus interruptus episode. "Understood."

The quiche were baking while the class started the sweet custard instructions. Jackie was working especially hard to give succinct instruction to her students. Mark admired her attention to detail. He knew he could instruct a class, whether he could make it informational and enjoyable at the same time was the question. More than once, he found himself trying to memorize a turn of phrase or statement she made. With no complications, she had the entire class making the clafoutis with ease. That she had given the instructions a lot of thought was clear. By the time the quiches were ready to come out of the ovens, the custards were ready to go in for their forty-minute baking time.

Jackie strolled around the room, praising her students individually for their quiches. Some of the students decided to taste test their creations, offering both Jackie and Mark samples. Most of the students had kept the ingredients simple, making tasty treats of fresh tomatoes and garlic or spinach and feta cheese. A few had overdone it with too many ingredients in one quiche, leaving them either undercooked or with soggy crust bottoms. Jackie gave each student a friendly critique. Mark did the same, more often than not parroting Jackie's comments because he couldn't find his own words of wisdom to relay.

As the forty-minute mark approached, Jackie gathered the students for instruction on how to test their clafoutis for doneness. "You want your testing pick to come out clean, and there should be a nice jiggle to the clafoutis. Nothing should look liquid."

Mark assisted his three rows of students as they each checked their bakes. Most found their bakes were done. As the ending time for the class was drawing near, students began to file out, taking their treats home. Neither Jackie nor Mark had a chance to taste test any of the clafoutis made that evening.

Walking out of the building after cleaning up, Mark decided to probe with a comment. "You're a real natural at this instruction business."

Jackie stopped in her tracks, perhaps at the suddenness of the compliment coming from him. "Thanks," she said, her eyes wary as if waiting for the bite of his next comment.

He had to admit, that was his modus operandi. But he was sincere. "Too bad it doesn't pay much doing it at community education."

"That's okay. I couldn't handle more than one class a week, considering my work schedule at the bakery."

"True, that would be difficult." He paused and cocked his head. "But what if you could do it full time?" Would she tell him about the job opening at King Mills Flour Company? Would she mention she was applying for a job as an assistant baking instructor?

Jackie hesitated, chewing her lower lip, her eyes darting side to side. Abruptly, she said, "Good night." Jackie turned back and headed for her car. Apparently not. There would not be any confessions from her. Not tonight anyway.

"Good night." Mark walked across the parking lot to his pickup truck. The entire time, his mind raced with questions. When was her interview? Was she still going to use the clafoutis instruction for her teaching presentation? Or would she use the quiche instruction which had been equally as good during this evening's class? Mark got in his truck and turned the key in the ignition. The engine roared. Mark shook his head. He had to get his brain in the game for himself. Tomorrow was his interview, and he didn't want to blow it worrying about Jackie and her performance.

CHAPTER THIRTEEN

"Jamaica's coming in with the baby!" Isabelle called into the kitchen.

Jackie stopped packaging the last of the Italian loaves in their plastic sleeves. Already a bit jittery over the interview this afternoon, her knees felt weak having to face her boss before running off to apply for a new job. She walked through the swing door in time to see Willow's stroller and her entourage come through the shop door and select a table.

Besides a smiling but tired looking Jamaica, in attendance was her father, Sydney Jones and his girlfriend, Mary Kettlebrook. Jackie stood back as a swarm rapidly developed around them. Staff and customers fawned over the blond infant sound asleep and oblivious to the audience she commanded. Aware the sales crew had abandoned their post, Jackie set up behind the sales counter until Isabelle, Jenny, and Vanessa returned. Only when the crowd had dissipated did she approach baby Caswell and her contingent.

Giving her boss a warm hug, Jackie said, "Thanks for coming to visit! It's so good to see you and meet Willow."

"I had to get out of the house. Four weeks, I was going crazy. I offered to take Dad and Mary to lunch so I could show off my baby. And thank everyone for the great baby gift." Jamaica patted the handle of the Chicco baby stroller the bakery employees had pitched in to buy.

Jackie bent over to get a look at the baby. Under a cap of pale blond wisps of hair, the round cheeky face of the tiny girl peered out from the cocoon of blankets, despite it being early June. Her big blue eyes took up most of her face while her coral pink little mouth puckered and pursed up.

Jamaica scrambled for the airplane carry-on sized diaper bag. She rummaged through it, pulling out a bottle of formula. "Oh, she's awake. Jackie, can you microwave this for twenty seconds please. Those faces mean she's hungry again and she's going to start wailing if we don't get this heated fast."

Doing as asked, Jackie hurried into the kitchen, returning minutes later just as Willow started to fuss. With the skill of a competent mother, Jamaica popped the bottle's nipple into the infant's mouth, silencing her crying. "Phew, that was close." She said, holding the end of the bottle. "She may be tiny, but she's got my lungs. She'd have cleared this place out if she got going good." The two women chuckled.

"Let me do that for you so you can socialize and eat your sandwich." Mary offered, taking control of the bottle.

Having relinquished feeding duty, Jamaica started to eat her BLT. "How's it going here? I haven't heard a word."

"Not bad. There's one thing I'd like to talk to you about."

She wiped her hands with the napkin and stood up. "Let's go back to my office. I need to find something there anyhow." In the office, Jamaica quickly found what she was looking for. "What's up?"

"Mark had a suggestion the other day about the temperature range in the storage room. He suggests we move the top range to less than fifty degrees so any insects that might be in the grain would remain dormant. It sounds like a smart idea. What do you think?"

Jamaica sat back in her desk chair. "Yeah, sure. Let's see how it goes. We haven't had any problems with the range as it is, but his point is valid." She rested her head against the chair back and closed her eyes. Jackie could see the dark circles and creases around her eyes. "By the way, I received notice of the next Downtown Merchant Association meeting. Can you cover for me, as my representative? It's June 17th at the VFW hall on Church Street. Seven o'clock."

"As long as it's not class night, I can make it."

"Good. Usually there's a fair number of women there. Just listen to what's going on and fill me in later. They're pretty boring but it's nice to meet up with some of the business people in town."

Jackie nodded. "Okay, I can do it. Maybe Regina and I can go together."

Jamaica gave her a long look. "Is there anything else?" Jackie hesitated. *Should I tell her about Mark's idea about sprouted breads and his market analysis? Maybe I should read the report myself first?* "Nope. That's it."

***

The single-storied, modern-styled structure had been designed to blend into the landscape, and it did. Driving up the winding road to the parking lot, Jackie marveled at the way it seemed nestled in among the surrounding trees. The parking lot abutted a meadow in the front of the building. It was a long walk to the building's entrance, and despite the beautiful smelling flowers, Jackie felt every step drawing her nearer to her destiny. The only fluttering butterflies she could concentrate on right now were in her stomach.

A quick right turn inside the doors brought her down a long hall to the baking school office, where she cordially greeted Mrs. Chester.

"Hello, I'm Jackie Thorndike. Here to see Mr. Goss," she said to the middle-aged woman at the reception desk.

"Hello, Miss Thorndike. Please have a seat in the waiting area." She gestured to the two chairs beside the wall near the window. "He'll be calling you shortly."

The ticking of a clock on the wall plucked at her nerves. It felt like hours. Jackie closed her eyes and ran through the steps of the teaching session in her brain. Step one, step two, step three; all the way through step eight. Good, everything was still with her.

The door at the end of the room opened, and a middle-aged, silver haired man stepped out to greet her.

"Ms. Thorndike. How nice to meet you," he said, shaking Jackie's hand after she stood up to greet him.

"Nice to meet you, Mr. Goss. Thank you for seeing me."

Frank Goss moved aside and gestured toward the door to his office. "Please, after you."

Jackie stepped ahead, leading the way back to the man's office. She took a seat in front of the hardwood desk while he sat down behind it.

"Let me start by saying, you have impressive references. Working at the best bakery in Boston for six years must have been quite an experience."

"Yes, it was. Especially since they milled their own flour. Getting to work with fresh flours brought out such amazing characteristics and flavors in the breads. It was fascinating."

"And yet, you left there for Jam Bakery. Not to say that it isn't a fine establishment, but why leave what some consider to be the best on the east coast for a brand-new small-town bakery?" Mr. Goss cocked his head to the side as he asked the question.

Jackie knew this question was going to come up and had prepared for the response. "I grew up in Putney, Vermont, so coming back to this state was coming home. Also, I knew independent bakeries in the area are also on a fresh-milled flour kick. Jamaica Jones's wanted to mill its own flour for their breads. She was looking for someone with experience to set up the milling and bread baking. I won the job."

"So, you run the flour milling and bread baking at Jam's? Single-handedly?"

"Yes, sir. Or I did until the owner, the pastry chef, went on maternity leave. Right now, I'm overseeing the entire operation and helping with pastry. But I'll be back to bread when Mrs. Jones-Caswell comes back to work." Jackie sucked in a breath. *Why are you rambling like a ninny? Stop it!*

"Your resume lists your attendance at the Northeast Culinary Institute Pastry Arts Program."

Jackie's breath held in her throat. "Yes sir." She crossed her fingers in her lap, then let out an inaudible sigh when he didn't ask why she wrote "attended" rather than "graduated."

"I also see you did an internship out of culinary school?"

"Yes, I interned for a year at Berkshire Bread Shop in Massachusetts. He also uses fresh-milled flours."

"Isn't he the guy who uses natural yeasts for his sourdoughs?"

"That's the one," Jackie said with a smile.

"Fascinating." He picked up her resume, letting his eyes skim the paper. "I see you are currently instructing an adult education class in baking. What topics do you teach?"

"I've taught bread, cake, and cookie baking. How to make different things with puff pastry. How to make quiche and custards. Next week we'll cover pâte à choux."

"That's quite an ambitious syllabus. How many students do you teach?"

"There are fifteen students."

"You do this single-handed?"

Jackie's heart sank. If only she could say yes. "I did initially but recently took on an assistant. A co-worker from the bakery helps me. Mainly, he assists half the class with the hands-on skills, while I do all the verbal instruction."

"I see," he said. "Well, let's go to the baking classroom and see how well you do."

Mr. Goss rose from his chair and led Jackie through a second door in the room that fed directly into the baking classroom.

"Would you like any props?" he asked before settling down on a high wooden stool.

"Yes, please. Two bowls, a whisk, and a pie plate, please."

Mr. Goss assembled the materials for Jackie, set them before her at the head instruction table, and resumed his seat in the audience area.

He pulled a notepad on the table before him closer, picked up a pen, and scribbled something. Glancing up, he smiled gently. "I may make notes during your presentation or move about the room. Please don't let that stop you."

Nodding, Jackie bit her lip. She touched each prop, moving each slightly.

"Whenever you're ready, Miss Thorndike."

CHAPTER FOURTEEN

Jackie walked out of the building feeling confident her presentation had gone well. Well enough anyway. She had momentarily forgotten the sixth step but quickly remembered and recovered. There was the time Mr. Goss had gotten up from his seat and walked to the back of the classroom, probably to find out if he could hear her there. Jackie had not stopped her session while he did this, and he seemed content. She must have been projecting well enough to be heard at the rear of the room. Nonetheless, his walking about the room reminded her to speak to the back of the room.

She got to her car, opened the passenger's side door, and dropped her handbag on the seat. As she slammed the door shut, she caught a glimpse of the front tire. It was flat.

Cursing under her breath, Jackie gave it a kick. Of all days to have this happen, it had to be when she was twenty-plus miles away from home and dressed in her best skirt and blouse. She tried to remember if she'd renewed her triple A membership. Unable to recall, she searched out her wallet, rummaging through it until she found her AAA card. It was expired. More curses resounded as she slammed the car door shut and headed for the trunk area of her old Subaru. She flipped open the lid and pulled out the temporary spare and the hardware she would need to change the tire herself.

Twenty minutes later, she removed the jack, placing the weight of the car on the spare, only to find it was flat as well. A streak of curses surrounded Jackie as she paced around the car. It was getting late. She was hungry, which didn't help the situation any. And more importantly, she didn't have enough spare cash or room on her credit card to hire a tow truck to take her to the nearest gas station for a tire repair.

Stumped as to what to do next, she leaned against the back of the Subaru and contemplated her options. She was scanning the much emptier parking lot for someone who looked like they might be able to help when she saw a familiar vehicle: a black Dodge Ram pickup quad cab. There was only one person she knew who owned such a vehicle—Mark Zutka. She turned toward the building just in time to see Mark exiting. *Crap. Mr. Nosey will want to know what I'm doing here. I wonder what he's doing here?* An uneasy feeling settled in her bones. *The best defense is a good offense.*

As if by some magical string, Mark looked over her way, spotting her. He stopped in his tracks when he saw her watching him. Then slowly, he resumed walking, this time heading her way instead of to his vehicle.

"What are you doing here?" Mark asked as he approached. His gaze roamed the tire-changing paraphernalia spread around her car.

Jackie stammered, "I came, uh, looking for a special ingredient. But, um, they didn't have it."

Mark smirked, "They have everything."

"Well, they didn't have rose water," Jackie huffed. "What are you doing here?"

Mark held up his left hand to show his shopping bag. "Shopping."

"Oh. For what?"

"A brotform and a new lamé." Mark frowned and quickly added, his arm gesturing toward the debris at her feet. "What happened?"

Jackie led him over to the side of the car and pointed. "I changed a flat, but the spare is also flat."

Mark stared for a minute, then handed Jackie his shopping bag. "Here, take this."

"Why?"

"Why must we play twenty questions? So I can grab your tire and throw it in my truck. I'll bring it to the nearest gas station to have it fixed, that's why."

"I'll come with you."

Mark hefted the tire and began walking to his vehicle. "Of course, you are. I'm not paying for this myself."

Deftly, Mark set the tire in the bed of his pickup while Jackie tucked the shopping bag in the back seating area of the cab. They both got in silently and Mark headed for the nearest gas station on the main road.

"Thanks for this," Jackie murmured, looking out the window. Her hands, white-knuckled, clutched her handbag in her lap.

"Seems I'm meant to always come to your rescue."

Jackie remained silent, her feet and knees held tightly together, her back stiff.

Mark shook his head and smirked.

The cab of the pickup was quiet as they drove the few miles into the center of town. In minutes, they pulled into the old-fashioned gas station. Two pumps occupied the small island, offering either gas or diesel, each pump having only one nozzle. Mark pulled through the pump lanes, parking the truck beside a used car for sale along the edge of the property.

"Wait here. It won't be but a minute or two." Hefting the tire out of the bed of his truck, he carried it over to the station office. Met at the door by an attendant no more than a teenager, the two began to converse. Mark set the tire down.

Jackie leaned her head back against the seat rest, her eyes glued to the side mirror, giving her a view of the encounter between the two males. From the gestures the kid was making, it wasn't going as planned. The gruffness of Mark's response filtered through the windows as the kid reddened, then pulled out his cell phone. After speaking with someone on the phone, the kid spoke with Mark again. Checking his watch, Mark nodded, and the kid stuffed his phone in his back jeans pocket. Leaving the tire on the asphalt, Mark stomped to the truck.

Shaking her head, her stomach in knots, she couldn't contain her anger. "What happened? What's going on with my tire?"

Sliding onto the driver's seat, Mark gripped the steering wheel, his knuckles white. He glanced away from her, across the street. "We have time to kill."

"What? Why? Are they going to fix it?" The vague response from Mark and his lack of explanation was churning her stomach even more.

"Because the only guy who repairs tires is out with the tow truck getting a disabled vehicle. He'll be back in about forty-five minutes."

Her eyes widened then she felt the sting of salty tears flooding them.

"The kid suggested we go chill across the street at the Murdock Inn. I'll buy you a beer or something. Whatever you want." He glanced across the street at the off-white two-story house. "Don't know about you, but I could use one, and I'll bet you could too."

Biting her lip to keep from crying outright, Jackie sniffled. "At the Murdock Inn? What are you suggesting?" She glanced past him across the street. The gabled facade held a full-length porch with a long row of rocking chairs. Flower boxes lined the edge of the porch, bursting with yellow, orange, and purple blossoms. It looked like the perfect place for a mint julep.

Mark rolled his eyes then sighed. "It's a drink. Only a drink. Until your tire is fixed."

"Okay."

They walked across the street, entering the historic 1700s house through the front door. Passing down the hallway, Jackie followed Mark to the entrance to the rather small bar. A few tables were filled. Only one couple sat at the far end of the bar, engrossed in conversation.

Choosing stools at the bar, they settled mid-way. The bartender immediately approached, setting a small menu card in front of them.

"I'll try the Whispering Pig ale," Mark said as he held out the menu to Jackie. Ignoring it, she winced at his brusque manner. "I'll have the same, please."

As the bartender started to turn away, Mark called out, "An order of eggplant fries, too."

"Please," Jackie added, giving Mark a stink eye and a side jab with her elbow.

Together, they watched the bartender disappear behind a door.

"I take it you've been here before."

Mark twisted his head to look at her. "I've been a few times. The brewery's next door. I've picked up a growler or two over the years."

Two pint glasses of amber ale were set down in front of them. Mark snapped his up and drank deeply. Taking a dainty sip, Jackie's insides eased as the cool, hoppy ale crossed her taste buds. "It's really good."

"Mm-hmm."

Jackie set her beer down. "I had a quick chat with Jamaica. She agrees with changing the temperature in the grain and flour storage room. I've lowered the temperature."

Mark twisted his head as if trying to catch every word. "Excellent. Thank you. I appreciate your having faith in my suggestion."

"You were right about the temperature range. It was too high." She felt a blush rising up her neck into her cheeks. *Or is it the beer getting to me already?*

Mark sat up straighter. "Did you give her the analysis?"

"No. It wasn't the appropriate time." She picked up her pint glass and stared down into it, unable to meet his eyes.

"I see. Do you know when you'll find" he used his fingers to air quote "an appropriate time?"

"No, I don't. Her visit today was a complete surprise." Jackie stared him down, the alcohol fueling her rebuke.

The bartender arrived with a pewter funnel-shaped dish holding eggplant fries and a small ramekin of dip. "Would you like to see the dining menu?"

"No—" Mark said.

"Yes—I would." Jackie interrupted, giving Mark another stink eye glance.

Her eyes skimmed the menu for the dining room in the Inn. "Wow, I love the menu. I'll have to come back for dinner someday. When I can afford it."

"The food is good. Both here in the bar and in the dining room." Mark added before taking a mouthful of fries.

Jackie looked away, heat rising at the sight of Mark's uncouth eating behavior. *At least he's not double-dipping in the remoulade sauce.* "I didn't notice the dining room when we came in."

"I don't think it's open just now. Though we're appropriately dressed for it." His eyes veered down to Jackie's skirt, hitched up as she sat, revealing half her thighs. "But we don't have a reservation or a room." His hand stroked down his tie.

Her mouth went dry while another part of her went warm. Too warm and wet. The overt gesture melted away the years. Back to their days and nights together during culinary school. When they had been friends and lovers. Back when they had trusted each other with their bodies and their dreams and their recipes.

The clank of Mark's empty glass hitting the bar top jolted her forward to the present. The bartender started forward to refill the glass, but Mark waved him off. "I'll go see if the tire is done yet. Be right back." He strode out the bar door, leaving her to sip at the warming beer and the cooling fries.

In a few minutes, he returned, his wallet in hand, and waved at the bartender to pay the bill.

"Tire's ready. We should get going." He jerked his head toward the door.

Taking one last sip, Jackie slid off the chair, her feet twisting beneath her as she crumpled toward the floor. Mark's burly arms surrounded her, lifting her up.

"Whoa, woman. You didn't drink more than a quarter of that glass, but are you sure you can drive?"

Shaking him off, she drew herself up ramrod straight. "I'm fine. That had nothing to do with the beer. Everything to do with these damn high heels."

"What are you doing with heels on, anyway?" Mark asked, a glimmer of a smirk on his face.

"Never mind." Jackie skirted by him for the door.

They drove back to her car in silence again.

Approaching her car, Mark said, "Let me put it on for you."

"No, you've done enough. I can do it. Besides, you're dressed too nice to be changing a tire."

"You're wearing a skirt, so let me do it. Besides, you've done it once already."

Jackie couldn't argue with either of these points, so she acquiesced and let Mark change out the repaired tire for the flat spare. He put the tools away in the car's trunk area and wiped his hands on the paper towel Jackie provided.

"There. You should be all set," he said, nodding toward the tire.

"Thanks. Thanks for everything. I guess I owe you again," Jackie said sheepishly.

"Someday, I'll call in the favor." Mark smiled as he shut the Subaru's rear door. He walked back to his own pickup and drove away as Jackie watched. Stunned at how amiable he'd been, she reminded herself Mark never did anything without a motive.

***

Her cell phone ringing startled her awake. Blurry eyed, she sat up on the couch and reached for it on the side table. Checking the time and caller ID, she was equally surprised to see it was two in the morning and the ID said it was the Fulton River Police Department. "Hello?"

"Miss Thorndike?" a female voice said.

"Yes? This is she."

"Hello, this is Dispatcher Justina at the Fulton River Police Department. We have an officer on patrol who reports a light on in the bakery. The doors are secure, but he wonders if you would wish to have the premises searched?"

Jackie blinked several times, trying to wrap her sleepy brain around the information. "A light on? That's not normal."

"That's what Officer Everett said. He also did not think the light was on during earlier passes this evening. Is there a lock box on the premises?"

"No, there isn't. Give me ten minutes, I'll be right down." Jackie said before shoving her feet into flip flops, grabbing her keys and purse, and heading out the door.

Spotting the police cruiser at the curb in front of the bakery, Jackie pulled up behind it. The officer walked over to her as she got out of the vehicle.

"There hasn't been any sign of movement inside. The light appears to be from the back area. Maybe the kitchen?" He said as they walked briskly up to the front door.

Peering inside, Jackie saw the light streaming out through the kitchen door into the sales area. The door was always propped open at night so that was not unusual. But all the lights should have been shut off. "It's coming from the kitchen area. All the lights should be off. Did you say the light hadn't been on earlier this evening?"

"That's right. Or at least I didn't notice it. But I walk the sidewalks around midnight after I come on shift. Look in on each store, make sure the doors are locked. That light wasn't on earlier." He stopped her when she reached for the door handle. "Give me the key, please, I'll enter alone and check it out. Just in case." Officer Everett held out his open palm.

"Okay. But let me know." She gave him the key and watched as he entered the store.

He looked around the front sales and dining area, a huge, heavy flashlight in hand, before approaching the open kitchen door cautiously. As Jackie watched, her nerves tingling with apprehension, he walked through the doorway and disappeared from sight, leaving an elongated shadow on the floor.

The shadow disappeared and for more minutes than Jackie cared to count, nothing happened.

At last, Officer Everett returned to the door leading someone before him.

Opening the door, Jackie let the two men pass, her heart in her throat. It was Mark, handcuffed, being led to the cruiser. "Wait. He works here."

"That's what he said. But he couldn't prove it."

"I can vouch for him." Jackie said to the officer. "Can you uncuff him, please?"

The entire time Mark had remained silent. Uncuffed, he rubbed his wrists before turning to the Jackie. "Thank you."

"Are we good here or are you going to press charges?"

"For what?" She searched between the two men, but both their faces were closed.

"He's intoxicated and he's on the premises after hours."

Jackie looked Mark up and down. He did look a little under the influence. "No. Thank you for all your help." Turning to Mark, she said, "Follow me." She walked back into the bakery, Mark following. "Have a seat. Give me a minute to get the lights."

After turning on one stretch of overhead lights in the dining area, Jackie and Mark sat down at a table. She looked at him, while he hung his head, refusing to meet her eyes. Like the time when she found him in his truck in the back parking lot, he was disheveled and stinking of alcohol. Hard anger flared in her chest as her lips tightened. Then just as suddenly, the wave was gone.

Sitting before her was Mark. Dealing with something that was overpowering him in ways she could not imagine. Mark, the invincible, as he used to call himself back when they spent so much time together, was letting something defeat him. Heading down a path of self-destruction. And from what she remembered from his family history; it was not a road she wanted to see him take.

"Mark. What were you doing here?"

He looked up, still not meeting her eyes. "I needed a place to sleep. I was sleeping on the locker room floor." He folded his hands in front of him on the tabletop.

Without thought, Jackie's hand reached out and cupped his fist. "Did your brother throw you out?"

"No. But he didn't want me in the cabin tonight." As if sensing her puzzlement, he quickly added, "It's date night."

Jackie closed her eyes and sat back in her chair. "I see. So, you couldn't go home."

"No. I had dinner out at O'Toole's, and then walked over here and curled up in the locker room for the night."

Mashing her lips together as she thought, Jackie nodded her head in understanding. An inner turmoil raged in her gut despite the calm veneer of her face. Bring him to her place? Or let him go back to the locker room? Looking him over again, she made her decision. "Come on with me, my couch is a little more comfortable than the locker room floor."

Mark's head shot up; his blood-shot eyes wide open. "You don't have to."

"I know." Jackie stood up. "Let's go."

***

The smell of brewing coffee woke him. The rich, deep fragrance made him think of French Roast, Jackie's favorite. It permeated the room Mark found himself in. White sheer curtains hung over the sliding glass doors. Sparsely furnished, the room had the couch he had been sleeping on, one rocking chair, and a bookcase he could tell was taller than him. There weren't any knick-knacky kinds of things hanging around. The only abundance was the bookcase, stuffed full of paperbacks and baking books. It overflowed onto the floor into half a dozen short stacks. Even the walls were spared of pictures or other accoutrements. The utilitarian setting made him sad for some reason. With the exception of the books, the minimalist appearance hinted at a life barely lived.

While he knew who he was with, he had no idea where he was and only vaguely remembered how he got there. The holes in his memory from last night left his gut even more unsettled than it usually was after a night of overindulgence.

"Good morning," Jackie's voice called out from around a corner into the next room Mark could only assume was the kitchen.

"Morning," he muttered as he sat up on the edge of the couch. "What time is it?"

"Half past nine."

Mark groaned and sank back down on the cushions.

Jackie appeared at his side. "None of that. Sit up." She held out a mug of coffee. "We have some things to discuss."

He slipped his hand into the mug handle and took a sip. "Oh God, so good. My brother can't make coffee. Not even the instant kind without ruining it."

Jackie settled on the couch beside him. "Let's talk."

Mark groaned again. "Please, I don't need a lecture."

"Oh, I'm not going to do the talking. You are."

"Me? Why me?" The unease in his gut started to churn with the addition of the dark roasted, acidic coffee.

"Look Mark, you've got something messing with your mind. You didn't have this problem back in baking school. What's going on?"

Staring down into his mug, Mark remained silent. *Where do I begin? How could she ever understand?* Yet as he thought that he knew her background was similar to his in some ways. She would understand.

"Come on, get some of it off your chest and shoulders so you can stand up taller instead of walking around hunch shouldered all the time."

After a long drink of coffee Mark sighed. "I'm becoming my father and I'm not happy about it. What else can I say?"

"How so? What makes you say that?"

"He drank a lot as I was growing up. Eventually it affected everyone. My Mom, us kids, his work. He was sick a lot. He went through a lot of jobs, couldn't keep any for more than a few months, sometimes only weeks or days." Mark paused. "By the time I was eight, he couldn't get anything. We lost our apartment and had to move into my maternal grandmother's house. My dad got really sick. Turned bright orange like a pumpkin and his abdomen swelled with fluid, like he was pregnant. The doctors told him to stop drinking but he wouldn't. He couldn't. He died of cirrhosis not long after.

Jackie's hand warmed his shoulder blade as she gently rubbed it. "I'm so sorry. It must have been a horrible thing to witness."

"It was. There was enough talk going on all the time, so I knew what was going on. Enough to understand he was killing himself with alcohol.

"Did you understand he couldn't help it? That alcoholism is a disease?"

"No. Not back then. I do now. And I see myself following in his footsteps. Unable to keep a permanent job, and binge drinking. I've tried to control it. Tried to only have one drink a day. But I'm not satisfied with one. I want another and another."

"Have you considered A.A. or Al-Anon?"

"No, I'm not a total drunkard."

Jackie chuckled softly and elbowed him lightly. "Mark, you're not a drunkard but as you yourself said, you have control issues. A.A. might be able to help you. Consider calling them or looking them up online."

Mark drained his coffee mug before meeting her eyes. "Okay. I'll check them out online. No promises."

"I'm not expecting or hoping for any." She patted his knee and stood up. "Breakfast coming up. Still like your eggs scrambled with ketchup?"

CHAPTER FIFTEEN

The phone rang a half dozen times. It stopped, then began ringing again. *Can't they get the hint? It's closed now.* The phone kept ringing. *Maybe the answering machine isn't picking up.* Annoyed, Mark slipped off his oven mitts and reached for the receiver.

"Hello, Jam Bakery," he said, finagling the phone between his ear and shoulder.

"Hello, I'd like to place a cake order for today if it's possible," a woman's voice said.

Mark looked at his watch. It wasn't yet six in the morning. Perhaps it was possible for Jackie to get the cake done if it wasn't too extraordinary. "What type of cake are you talking about?"

"I need a simple two-tier yellow birthday cake, enough for six to eight people. And I'd like to pick it up at three o'clock this afternoon."

"Well, we close at three, so if you can pick it up sooner, you can have your cake," Mark replied, mentally finishing the phrase with *and eat it too.*

"That's fine. I can do that. Please write on the cake, 'Happy Birthday Harold.' His birthday isn't really until June twelfth, but two days earlier isn't too early, don't you think?" the woman asked before giving her name as Milly Parks.

"No, not at all. Any special designs or colors, Mrs. Parks?"

"Make the decoration frosting blue against a white frosting. That will be good enough for Harold."

"Great," he said, "we'll see you this afternoon."

Mark hung up the telephone receiver and began searching for a piece of paper and pencil or pen to write down the order. As he was doing so, the timer on the oven sounded.

Cursing, Mark left the desk area and went to remove the loaves of French bread from the ovens.

***

The door swung open, and Isabelle Becker stepped into the kitchen that afternoon. She spotted Jackie at the pantry door and rushed over. "I'm sorry to bother you, but do you have Mrs. Parks' birthday cake done yet? She's here to pick it up."

Jackie set aside her supply clipboard and stared at Isabelle, her eyes wide and wary. "What cake order? I didn't have a cake order today."

Isabelle shuffled her feet side to side. "There's a woman out front who says she ordered a cake. I don't see any cake with the correct inscription on it."

Checking the order clipboard hanging on the wall, they did not find any order for a birthday cake.

The two women looked at each other. Jackie sighed and headed for the front sales counter.

There stood an elderly woman dressed in her Sunday best, waiting.

Jackie strode up to the counter before the woman and asked, "How can I help you, Mrs. Parks?"

The woman clutched her handbag tighter and set it on the countertop. "I've come to pick up the cake I ordered, but your helper can't seem to find it."

"I'm sorry, but we didn't have an order for a cake for you today," Jackie said, trying to be as sensitive to the woman's plight as possible. Clearly, she had a big problem if she thought she'd ordered a cake and really hadn't.

"I ordered the cake myself. Blue icing on white. 'Happy Birthday Harold' is what it should say."

"When did you order the cake?" Jackie asked.

"I got up early this morning, and it was the first thing I did; call here and order the cake."

A sick feeling began to blossom in the pit of Jackie's stomach. "What time was that?"

"It must have been about five or five fifteen this morning. I was surprised you were open so early. I thought I was going to have to leave a message, but you don't have an answering machine."

Jackie turned to Isabelle, and the two women stared at each other in silent communication.

"I'm sorry, Mrs. Parks, but there has been a mix-up, and your order was never recorded. We don't have a cake ready for you."

Isabelle walked away to the cooler and returned with a two-tiered layer cake with multi-colored frosting roses, green leaves, and yellow decorative icing on white. She held it up for Mrs. Parks to see.

"We do have this cake available, if you would like it," Isabelle offered, chewing on her bottom lip.

"No, that won't do," Mrs. Parks said. "I wanted blue on white. And no roses."

"I'm afraid, that's all I have to offer you. I could make you a cake for tomorrow, or you can have this cake today at half price."

Mrs. Parks looked from Jackie to Isabelle, her mouth slammed shut, lips barely visible, and eyes fuming. "I can't change the party to tomorrow. I'll have to take the cake."

"What shall I write on it? 'Happy Birthday Harold,' is that correct?" Isabelle asked.

"Yes, that's right." Mrs. Parks said, opening her purse and removing her wallet.

Jackie reached for the woman's credit card and rang up the sale while Isabelle wrote out the words on the cake top. She quickly placed the cake into a cake box and handed it over to Mrs. Parks, who swiftly left the store in a huff.

Both women watched her leave, then stared at each other. There was only one person in the shop at that hour this morning, and he wasn't here now. But he'd hear about the problem he'd caused as soon as Jackie could get to him.

CHAPTER SIXTEEN

A note attached to Mark's locker alerted him that something was up. Jackie wanted to speak with him when she got in that morning. That gave Mark a total of two hours to brood over what the subject of her discussion could possibly be.

At first, he hoped maybe he was going to get a raise. He'd been on the job for weeks now; it wasn't that unlikely he would merit an increase in salary so soon, considering how low his starting wage was.

But then, Mark had a gut feeling that he'd done something wrong, but he couldn't figure out exactly what he'd done. He tried to think back over yesterday's work and decided he'd made everything according to the recipes. Despite wanting to change a few things, he'd left things alone and done his job as prescribed.

Today, however, was a new day. And if he was going to get yelled at for doing one thing wrong, he might as well get yelled at for two.

Mark's first order of business was to make the ten dozen grinder rolls for the two pizza joints in town: Tony's Pizza and Gianni's Ristorante. He pulled out the Jam Bakery recipe binder and looked up the recipe. Then he slammed the binder shut and put it back on the shelf.

Pulling an index card out of his pants pocket, he started to make the grinder rolls using his own recipe instead of the official recipe of the Jam Bakery. His recipe called for few ingredients and had a softer crumb with tiny air bubbles, unlike the official recipe that had a tough crumb and larger air bubbles. It was almost like comparing Italian bread to ciabatta bread. Mark was sure the restaurant owners would like his version of the rolls better. Besides, his recipe had won the praise of his instructors at pastry arts school.

Two hours later, Mark was separating the finished rolls into their plastic bins for the two different restaurants. Tony's took seven dozen, while Gianni's bought the rest, each day. He couldn't wait to hear back from the restaurant owners over the change in the rolls. In an hour, they would be delivered to their respective owners for today's use.

Just as he was finished packaging the rolls, Jackie walked into the kitchen through the back door.

"Hey," Mark said. "Good morning."

Jackie walked over toward him. "Good morning, so far," she said, setting down her handbag on the kitchen table. "We need to talk a minute."

* * * *

Mark ambled over to the table and pulled out a chair. "Okay," he said, sitting down. "What's up?"

Pulling out a chair, Jackie sat down also. "We had an incident yesterday. Perhaps you can shed some light on what happened?"

Mark's brow furrowed. "I doubt it but shoot."

"Mrs. Parks arrived yesterday afternoon to pick up a birthday cake only to find that we had never made one for her. We, or should I say, I, never got the order for it."

The expression on Mark's face said it all. In a rush, the memory of the telephone call from Mrs. Parks came flooding back to him. He remembered taking the order but couldn't remember writing it down.

"That's what I thought," Jackie said, her shoulders stiff and her eyes flashing. "I thought maybe you had taken the order and somehow forgot to pass it along to me."

"I'm sorry," he said. "The phone kept ringing and ringing. The answering machine wasn't picking up."

Jackie's eyebrows knitted. "I'll have a look at it. But still, you should have written the order down."

"I know, I forgot. Or I tried to, but the oven timer went off, and I chose to remove the loaves before they burned instead of writing it down. Then I just plain forgot."

"Well, it was pretty embarrassing to have to deal with Mrs. Parks yesterday. From now on, you write down every order and hand it off to me or Isabelle when we get in. No excuses. The bread won't burn that quickly that you can't write down the instructions in a few minutes."

"Okay, okay. I get it. I'll write down everything that's called in." Mark said, raising his hands in surrender.

"Good. I know it doesn't happen often, but it's important."

Mark frowned. "Would you stop whipping the dead horse?"

"As long as I've been clear enough—" Jackie started to say.

"Absolutely clear. Let it go."

"Fine." Jackie picked up her handbag and started for the locker room. "That's screw-up number one. Consider this a verbal warning."

Watching her disappear across the kitchen and through the locker room door, Mark sat silent and waited. He turned toward the bins containing the grinder rolls and smiled. She'd be happy when those restaurant owners praised the new, finer rolls. And he'd be out of trouble.

CHAPTER SEVENTEEN

It wasn't long after Mark left for the day at eleven-thirty in the morning that the first problem was brought to her attention.

Once again, Isabelle came to get her from the front of the shop. "Sorry, Jackie, but we have a problem. Tony De Motta is here about the grinder rolls," she said with a pained expression on her face.

Jackie's heart sank. She walked into the salesroom and stepped up to the counter to speak with Mr. De Motta. "Tony, what seems to be the problem?"

Mr. De Motta held out a hand with two grinder rolls clenched in it. He set them both on the countertop. "The grinder rolls I received today are all wrong. They can't stand up under the weight of the ingredients. Especially the wet ones. Once you put oil or vinegar or tomato sauce on the inside, the crumb collapses into mush." He broke open one roll. "See, this is one roll leftover from yesterday. This is how it should look." He broke open the second roll with his fingers. "And this—this is what you delivered today. No good."

Jackie picked up the first roll and examined it. The crumb was hard and irregularly pocked with medium-sized air bubbles like Ciabatta bread. She picked up the second roll. The crumb was soft with a fine texture like Wonder Bread. "I see your point. Are you sure you received them from us?"

"Absolutely certain. I have seven dozen rolls I can't do anything with, and I have nothing to make grinders with today. I can't work with these. Any chance you have some of the right kind left?"

"No, I'm sorry," she said, rubbing her forehead. "I don't have any left over from yesterday. I will make you a new batch right now, but it will take two hours to get them to you."

"That means I'll miss filling grinder orders over lunch. But that's better than not having any at all. Please make me some new rolls."

"I'll do that and have them delivered as soon as they're ready," Jackie said, taking the two sample rolls and setting them in a paper bag.

Tony nodded his thanks and returned to his own shop next door.

Jackie picked up the phone and called Gianni's Ristorante. "Is Gianni available please, it's Jackie Thorndike over at Jam Bakery calling about the grinder rolls," she said to the person who answered.

When Gianni Vespucci was on the phone, Jackie said, "Mr. Vespucci, I'm sorry about the rolls you were sent this morning. Are you having trouble with them?"

"It's as if you read my mind. I was going to call you. They're terrible. They don't hold up. They're turning to mush as we make the sandwiches."

"I know, we've had a problem. We must have used the wrong recipe this morning. I will replace them within two hours. I know that doesn't help you with lunch service, but at least it will get you through the rest of the day. And it won't happen again."

"I hope you are right. I would hate to have to find another supplier. Please hurry," was all he said before hanging up.

Two and a half hours later, Jackie was personally delivering new rolls to Tony De Motta and Gianni Vespucci.

Fifteen minutes after returning to the shop, instead of going home, as was her normal schedule, Jackie was on the telephone in Jamaica's office calling Mark.

"Hello," he said.

"Mark, it's Jackie. We've had another incident. No make that two, but they're related so we'll consider it one," she said.

"What now?"

"What recipe did you use for the grinder rolls this morning? Because it certainly wasn't the one you were supposed to be using."

"I, uh, used one from baking school."

"Really. And who gave you the authority to change the recipe?"

Mark stammered, "No one. I decided they deserved something better."

"Better? Not for grinders. Your rolls fell apart under the wet toppings."

Mark was slow to respond. "Oh. I hadn't thought of that."

"Well, let me tell you, I've just finished baking a replacement batch with the correct recipe and delivering them to Tony's and Gianni's. We're lucky they are still willing to purchase from us after that fuckup. Don't ever change a recipe without authorization again. Do you understand?"

The phone was silent for a few seconds before Mark said, "I get it."

"Good. That's incident number two. Don't let number three happen or you are history, Mark. Do you hear me?"

"I got it."

"Excellent." She slammed down the receiver on the phone hook.

CHAPTER EIGHTEEN

A bell jingled as she walked through the front door. The powerfully sweet fragrance of gardenias encircled her like a warm crocheted afghan. Undertones of wet peat, greenery, tulips, daffodils, and hyacinths added to the perfume.

Regina Maxwell passed through green velvet curtains into the front of the shop from a back room. "Hi Jackie, what a surprise. Is this your first time here?"

"Yes, since the renovation."

"Renovation? That's putting it mildly. Total makeover is more like it," she laughed. "I had to gut the store down to studs and throw everything out after the hurricane."

"Hurricane Mindy had most everyone on this street doing that. That's how Jamaica got her bakery."

"At least Jamaica and I had insurance to cover our damages and rebuilding. Some folks didn't and lost everything, including their businesses."

Bending over to sniff at a jasmine flower, Jackie inhaled deeply, her eyes closed, her smile radiant. "There wasn't much help, was there? I would have thought the Downtown Merchant Association would have been more helpful for the business owners."

Gina rolled her eyes, her head shaking. "Oh, the men were a great help to each other. It was every *woman* business owner for herself."

Frowning, Jackie shook her head in sympathy. "Figures." She walked around the shop, the greenery and blossoms lifting her spirits. "But you made out okay?" She fingered an asparagus fern hanging from the ceiling.

"Well, the insurance was a battle. But I got enough to renovate between the insurance money and a bank loan. I had to buy used flower coolers instead of new. But I'm open, and that's all that counts right now."

"It looks and smells marvelous in here." She looked up at the hanging plants. "Maybe I should buy some for the bakery? You know, hang them in the front window?"

"That would look great. Give it a homey feeling." Regina stepped forward to pull one down.

"Let me check with Jamaica first."

"Right, of course. Did you need anything in particular?"

"Just an escape."

Regina put the plant back up on its hanger. "Oh, dear. Mark again?"

Jackie nodded. "You know, I can understand forgetting to write down an order. Everyone at the bakery has done it once. But this time, he deliberately used his own recipe to make grinder rolls for Tony's Pizza and Gianni's Restaurant." She shook her head. "They couldn't hold up to the ingredients, so I had to remake both orders pronto. Sixteen dozen rolls."

"Oh my! I hope he learned his lesson."

"Me too. It was an expensive one for the bakery. If he does it again or steps any toe out of line for any reason, he's fired. Jamaica has a strict policy of consistency. Everything is strictly controlled for it."

Regina put her arm around Jackie and squeezed gently. "Forget about it now. Clear your mind. How are Jamaica and the baby? What did she and Ronnie name her?"

"I haven't called lately. I'm trying to give Jamaica a break from the bakery, though she stopped in for a visit a week or so ago. Last I knew, everyone was doing great. The baby's name is Willow Debra Caswell. Debra was Jamaica's mother's name."

"Hmm, Willow. That's different. I like it."

"Me too. And—" Jackie's phone rang. She checked the screen, held up her index finger, and answered the call. "Yes—okay, I'll be right there."

"Not another Mark problem, I hope." Regina chuckled.

Jackie smirked. "Not this time, thank God. But I have to go. Can we get together some Saturday for dinner? Maybe The Dockside Restaurant?"

"Love that place. Sounds great. Let me know when you're free."

The incident today had thrown Jackie off-kilter. It still wasn't five o'clock yet by the time she hit O'Toole's, but she didn't care. It was close enough, and she badly needed some alcohol to wash away today's escapades. Pat made her a stiff Manhattan; she downed half of it in one gulp. She ordered a plate of buffalo wings and one of mozzarella sticks for dinner and sat on her barstool watching the clock tick.

As soon as the food arrived, she dug in, feeling hungrier than she had in weeks and needing to get something in her stomach to soak up the alcohol. She sat minding her own business, trying not to think about work and failing miserably.

What had gotten into Mark lately that he could screw up so royally? He was the only one to remember her birthday—and give her a present. He'd been kind enough to help her at King Mills with the flat tire. Why was he acting so passive-aggressive? Didn't he feel like part of the team? Sure, his position was temporary, but still, he *was* part of the team. Why couldn't he leave everything the way it was and just follow orders. Why screw up the cake order? How hard was it to write down 'Happy Birthday Harold' and 'blue/white' on an order slip?

Jackie spun her chair around when she heard her name being called. It was Brent McCormick, an old-time local and frequent flyer at all the bars in town, coming over to talk with her. Maybe he'd be able to get her out of the work-funk and onto a different train of thought.

"Hey, Jackie. How are you?" Brent slid onto the barstool beside her.

"Good, Brent. How about you?" Jackie set down her chicken bone and wiped her fingers clean on a napkin.

"I was wondering if you knew if Mark heard back from King Mills yet?"

Jackie sat up straight. "What about King Mills?"

"Well, you know, the interview and all. How'd he do?" Brent asked, signaling Pat for a beer.

It all came flooding back to her. The dress jeans, the button-down dress shirt, the jacket, that day at King Mills when she had her interview.

"Is Mark trying for a job at King Mills Flour?" Jackie sat up straighter as her pulse began to race uncontrollably.

"That's what he said at the Whiskey Den last weekend." Brent cocked his head. The look on his face got a little queer. "Oops, maybe I wasn't supposed to say anything."

No wonder the man was there on the same day as she interviewed. He'd been there for an interview too. And the slime-ball had tried to cover his tracks with a purchase, probably just in case he ran into her.

"No, that's okay. I figured it out anyway," Jackie said. "What job did he apply for? Was it the baking instructor's job? Jackie felt her face get hot as her blood started to boil.

"Yeah. So, he hasn't heard back from them yet?" Brent inquired, lifting his beer bottle up to the light.

"No, I don't think they've decided yet."

"Too bad. I hope he finds out soon. I know he really wants the job. Being permanent with bennies and all."

"True."

"Well, great talking with you." Brent picked up his bottle and walked back to the cluster of guys he'd been hanging out with earlier.

Jackie held up her near-empty glass to Pat, "I'll have another."

CHAPTER NINETEEN

The next morning, Isabelle approached Jackie in the kitchen where she stood packaging cooled loaves of ciabatta bread. "We have a problem developing."

Looking up, she saw the concern etched on her co-worker's face. Her own gut started to clench tighter at the impending news. Setting aside the unfilled bag in her hands, she asked, "What's happening?"

"The refrigerated bakery case in the salesroom isn't quite within temperature range for the second consecutive day. And it's making a funny noise. I think it's going to die."

The two women walked to the unit in the salesroom where Jackie reviewed the temperature chart on a clipboard.

"Looks like it's been fading for a week. But you're right. It's probably getting dangerously close to being unserviceable."

Handing the clipboard back to Isabelle, Jackie nodded. "Can you check it four times a day now? I'll have Mark check it when he gets in at three; I'll check it again at six. Can you check it at noontime and at closing time?"

"Sure."

"I'll call the repair service and see what they have to say."

In Jamaica's office, she called the appliance service. Despite her insistence, they didn't want to come out unless it was an emergency. After much dickering, Jackie was able to make an appointment for a 'preventative maintenance' the following week.

Relaying the information to Isabelle, the woman shook her head. "Figures. They're hoping it will die before then so they can charge us for an emergency call. Don't worry. I'll keep a close watch on it. Between the three of us, we should know as soon as it dies."

"Let's be cautious and put all our products in the kitchen walk-in refrigerator overnight."

Mark found the refrigerated case dead when he arrived at 3 am. Jackie still had to clean out the inside before the appliance service would touch it. They gave it a cursory look before determining the unit's compressor had broken, and the unit was so old it wasn't worth repairing.

Time to call Jamaica. Jackie sat at Jamaica's desk, feeling uncomfortable in the deeply cushioned desk chair. It was the only luxury the owner allowed herself. "Jamaica, it's Jackie. The refrigerator case died."

What the repair service had said didn't surprise her boss. "It's so old. He whined to me about fixing it the last time I called him in. Said he had a hard time finding parts." Jamaica sighed. "Can you try to find a used replacement?" Her voice got anxious. "I'm sorry, I can't do it. My hands are full right now."

Jackie's eyelids shut as her head drooped, "Yes, of course I can. No problem." She disconnected the call, her mind racing. *Where the hell do I find a used refrigerated pastry case?*

Sitting back in the chair, her eyes closed, her brain scurried for an answer. The visit she had to Regina's shop came to mind. She picked up the phone and dialed. "Regina, I need a new refrigerator case for pastries. Any suggestions?"

"I've got just the supplier for you," Regina said, the smile on her face evident in her voice.

By late afternoon the next day, a used refrigerator pastry case was delivered to Jam Bakery while Jackie and Regina watched from a table in the dining area.

"I can't believe how quickly that all came together." Jackie took a sip of her iced chai tea.

Regina looked smug. "It's all in who you know."

Jackie was quiet a minute. "You know what I think. This is what the Downtown Merchant Association should be helping its members with—business problems. Not sucking us dry every single month collecting for flags on telephone poles or new uniforms for peewee soccer."

Regina looked at her, an astonished look in her eyes.

"Oh, don't get me wrong. I guess those are worthy causes. But I expected a merchant association would help each other: networking, referrals, strategic partnerships. Not arguing for half an hour whether their high school yearbook ad should be a full page or half and what color the background should be."

"Hmm. You have a huge point there." Regina crossed her arms over her chest. "How many times have we women asked the board of directors and officers to go after the town to set up public bathrooms at the Fulton River Falls Park, so the tourists don't leave to find a bathroom and never come back to shop?"

"Exactly. Every time we suggest something, it's ignored. Or worse, we're patronized."

The women huddled together. Jackie whispered, "Tomorrow is the next meeting, and it's an election of officers. I suggest we submit our own slate of officers."

"Who do you think would do it?"

"Maddie Dailey is very outspoken about the lack of facilities for mothers. And both her kids are in school now. I bet she could be persuaded to run for president."

"How about you for VP?"

"I'd rather be secretary. Why don't you take the VP job?"

Regina bit her lip. "Well, okay. I don't think the VP does much. Who do you think we can get to run for treasurer?"

"How about Elowen Sparke at Sparkle Jewelers? She's pretty outspoken about issues too. I could stop by and talk to her after I finish up here."

"Great idea. I'll visit with as many of the women along Main Street as I can. Let them know what we're up to."

"Perfect. Those men will never know what hit them."

PROOF OF LOVE

The two women raised their coffee cups in silent salute as the new refrigerated case came on line.

CHAPTER TWENTY

Jackie had bit her tongue for two days. There was too much going on with the dead product case and all. She so wanted to say something to Mark, to let him know that she was on to him. But she didn't. It nearly killed her to say nothing, but she didn't want to let on that he and she were possibly in competition for the same job.

Mark knew something was up. He kept looking over at her as she worked, a puzzled expression on his face. *Good, let him wonder. He probably thinks it has everything to do with the equipment failure.* She went about her baking as though he wasn't even there.

By that third morning, Mark looked frazzled.

Jackie, too, was feeling smug but tired of the farce. Her nerves were wearing thin, trying to sidestep around Mark in the kitchen.

"What's so funny?" Mark interrupted her thoughts.

"What? Nothing." Jackie replied, trying desperately not to blurt out what she knew.

"That smile didn't look like nothing. Tell me what's rolling around that head of yours." Mark egged.

Jackie snapped. "You want to know what I'm thinking? I'm thinking you're a real shit for applying for the King Mills Flour job opening."

"What? How—? Who told you?" Mark stammered; his eyes widened with shock.

Jackie spun around to face him directly. "What does it matter? I know. Did you know I was going for the same position?"

Mark nodded.

All the pent-up venom sputtered out of her. "You're such an asshole. I can't believe you would do such a thing."

"Can't believe I'd want a permanent position with benefits and a pension? Are you kidding? Look at me. I'm twenty-eight years old and still jumping job to job. I want something permanent. I deserve something permanent, with benefits." He pointed one floury thumb at his chest.

"Did you have to go for the same job?"

"Yes, I did. King is a great employer. Who wouldn't want to work for them?"

"Enough." She raised her hand. "I've heard enough. I don't want to argue with you. It's too late to do anything about it unless you're willing to withdraw your application."

Mark looked at her as if she'd asked him to detach his own head. "Not a chance. I've heard enough too." Mark grumbled and headed into the salesroom.

"Never mind," Jackie retreated toward the locker room, the steam still rushing from her ears.

***

The second Mark entered the salesroom, he was sorry he did. Customers were lined up three and four deep at the counter, all vying for the last of the morning's pastries.

"Great, Mark, you're here. I could use your help," Isabelle said as she handed over the change to a customer along with a white box of goodies.

"Not what I came in here for," Mark said, hands on his hips.

"Please, Mark." Isabelle's pleading eyes reached out to him.

Mark sighed, then grabbed a white box and turned back toward the counter. "Who's next?"

Two hands shot up in the air, one belonging to an elderly woman, the other belonging to a fifty-something-year-old man in a business suit.

"I was here first," the woman said, shoving forward toward the counter's edge.

"Like hell, lady," the man replied, also driving forward until he stood beside her.

Mark watched as the two customers battled it out. His blood pressure, which was already high after the altercation with Jackie, was now close to boiling point. "When you two decide who's first, let me know, and I'll be happy to assist that person," he said through clenched teeth.

"It's me!" The woman called out.

"Forget her; it's me," the man bellowed.

Stepping back and folding his arms across his chest, Mark leaned against the bread case behind him. It was getting entertaining watching the two customers go toe to toe. He smirked, watching them.

"Look, shit-face. I'm next. Give me a dozen pastries to go and hurry. I've got a meeting at the office in twenty minutes," the man called out to Mark.

Mark's smile fell. "What did you call me?" He stood up straight, feet spread wide apart, shoulders back.

"Never mind that. Get me those pastries."

"You want pastries? I'll get you pastries," Mark said as he opened the sliding back of the pastry case. He reached in and selected a lemon curd puff pastry square. "How about this? Will one of these do?" He held it out on the palm of his hand.

"Yeah, that's great. I'll have two of those and three of the strawberry, plus a couple apricot and five cherry." The man busied himself reaching for his wallet in his back right pocket.

"Okay, bud. Here's your pastry." Mark picked up another lemon curd in his free hand and flung both frisbee-style at the man, striking him in the side of the head.

The man looked up just in time for the launch of two strawberry pastries. This time he ducked in time, and the pastries sailed over his head into the crowd behind him.

"Hey, what the fuck do you think you're doing?" the man roared.

Mark gave him a wicked smile. "Getting you your order." He reached down, pulled out two cherry pastries, and let them fly. This time the man wasn't so quick, and the pastries struck him in the center of his chest, leaving smears of cherry on his white shirt and tie.

The man bellowed again as Mark continued to fling pastries at him, striking him in the chest and head. Finally, the man lunged across the counter, grabbing a handful of Mark's apron. Mark took a swing at him, but the man ducked out of the way.

"What is going on here?" Jackie yelled over the din. She had rushed through the swinging door in time to see the two men grappling.

Both men came to a standstill, finally letting go of each other before returning to their own side of the counter.

"Mark—locker room." Jackie bellowed through teeth clenched so tight it was almost difficult to understand what she said.

Mark turned away from the salesroom and left through the kitchen door fuming all the way. It was that asshole's fault. He deserved what he got, the arrogant bastard. Mark stomped through the kitchen into the locker room and sat down on one of the chairs in front of his locker. He untied his apron and flung it into the dirty laundry bin. *Just what I need, yet another lecture from the thorn in my side.*

CHAPTER TWENTY-ONE

Jackie paused at the entrance to the locker room. It had taken twenty minutes to get the crowd settled in the front salesroom. Mr. Stewart had left in a huff screaming about his dry-cleaning bill. Mrs. Tiggans and the remaining customers were titillated at the scene they had just witnessed. Jackie had helped Isabelle restore order, clean up the mess, and waited on a few customers before leaving to deal with Mark.

What should she do about Mark? Her heart sank and the pit of her stomach churned. *What about Mark's alcohol problem? Would this push him into another binging episode?* Her hands scrubbed her face. *I can't think about that. That's not my problem. The bakery has to be my focus. It has to be my priority.*

There was no question what she would have to do about Mark, for the good of the bakery. She only hoped Jamaica would understand. This had nothing to do with Mark going for the same job she wanted at KMF. It had everything to do with his lack of appropriate customer service. Between the cake and the grinder roll issues, she had given him another chance. But this food fight with the customer. One of their regular customers at that. Mark was going to have to pay for his mistakes now. There was no other way.

A part of Jackie was sorrowful that it had come to this. Mark wasn't such a bad guy. He made bad choices, yes, but he didn't deliberately set out to harm anyone. Well, except for this time with Mr. Stewart. Jackie had been told the incident was provoked by Mr. Stewart, but still. Mark should have had sense enough to ignore the comment or at least walk away. Not get into a brawl with a customer.

She sighed heavily before pressing into the door. It swung open to reveal a slumped Mark sitting on a chair in front of his open locker. He had already changed into his street clothes. He knew what was coming.

"Mark, I'm sorry I have no choice left," Jackie said after coming to stand beside him.

"Don't bother." Mark slammed the door shut on his empty locker.

Jackie shifted her weight between her feet. "I can't overlook that behavior."

"I said, don't bother. I'm well aware of the issues."

She rested her hand on his shoulder, but he instantly shook it off. "I just want you to know this has nothing to do with the job opening at KMF."

"It may not, but you're not missing a legitimate reason to fire me, are you?" He sneered, venom in his voice.

Jackie steeled her posture. "We can't have these kinds of mistakes and behaviors here."

"I get it. Don't worry. I won't dally," he said, picking up his backpack and heading for the door.

As Jackie watched, Mark disappeared out the locker room door without another word. A rush of air exhaled from her lungs as she slumped onto the chair Mark had vacated. The problem was gone; she should feel relieved. But had she wronged him again?

Her mind skipped back eight years to the day everything between them went wrong.

Using her key card, Jackie opened the student baking lab door at the Northeast Culinary Institute. As she had been doing every afternoon at five o'clock for the last month, she came to feed her natural yeast sourdough starter. Taking her jar off the shelf, she opened it.

The smell hit Jackie first. Her head recoiled away from the jar. Instead of the tangy, cheesy smell her sourdough starter had yesterday, the smell today was like rotting meat.

Peering through the quart canning jar, she noticed pinkish-orange streaks on the surface of the bubbly, beige starter.

"No! No! No!" Jackie yelled, dropping her forehead to the tabletop, her eyes closed, spilling tears.

"What's wrong?" a male voice called out from across the room.

Jackie didn't have to look to recognize Paul Drexell. "My sourdough is contaminated. There isn't enough time to make new starter." Her heart raced with the implications.

"Let me see." Paul took the jar and peered inside. "Shit, yeah. This is no good. What are you going to do?"

Jackie's tears poured down her face. She buried her head in her arms. "Two years of my life and sixteen thousand dollars wasted in one bad sourdough starter. I can't use that for the final examination. I'll flunk." She stumbled over to the nearest chair and sat down. "I was top of the class." Not wanting to break down completely in front of Paul, she turned away; her heart aching and wretched with what could have been if only her starter were still usable.

After a few minutes, she noticed Paul stood looking at her, a weird expression on his face. It piqued her curiosity. Sniffling and wiping her cheeks of tears, she mumbled, "What?"

"I have an idea," Paul said, going to the shelf where all the students' sourdough jars were stored. He took one down. "Here, take half of this."

Blurry as they were with tears, her eyes popped wide open. "That's cheating. We were each supposed to create our own wild sourdough starter and use it to make our last projects next week."

Paul sidled up beside her, put his arm around her shoulders, and squeezed lightly. With a lowered voice, he said, "True. But who's going to know. Unless someone walks in right now." Paul placed the jar on the table. "Besides, I'm here to feed my starter. Which means I'm throwing half of it away and adding more flour. Which is what I suspect you were here to do to yours too, right?"

Jackie nodded, her tears slowing.

"So, take my discard. It's not much, but if you feed it twice a day over the weekend, you'll have enough to do your final projects next week." Paul gave her a megawatt smile. "Problem solved. And no one is the wiser."

"Why are you helping me? I thought you didn't like me." Jackie's eyes narrowed, and her gut clenched uneasily.

"I was jealous. You and Mark have been quite the item lately. I'm jealous I can't spend as much time with him. He and I used to hang out a lot until you came around."

Eying him and biting her lip, Jackie contemplated the offer. If she didn't accept it, she would flunk out of the Northeast Culinary Institute's prestigious Professional Baking and Pastry Arts Program. If she did take it, she could finish and graduate. But if her deceit came to light, she'd be thrown out, a disgrace she didn't want to face or write on her resume.

She looked around. There weren't any closed-circuit cameras. No one else was in the room. She went to the equipment shelf and got a clean jar.

Paul held the jar steady as she scooped half the contents into the new jar. She quickly labeled it as her previous jar had been labeled and put it in the old jar's place on the students' shelf.

As she dumped the contents of her old jar, Paul stood aside, watching.

"Brava. I think you made the right decision. Now get out of here."

Her legs shook as she headed for the door. Turning back when she reached it. "Thank you, Paul. You're a real pal."

"Shhh. Don't tell anyone. Not even Mark." Paul held his finger to his lips, then shooed her away with his hand.

As she headed out the door, her nerves tingled. Paul had not added more flour to his jar, only replaced it on the shelf.

She blinked back tears at the memory. The following days had been full of accusations: by Mark, who found half his starter gone, and by Paul, who had told everyone he caught her stealing Mark's starter. An investigation quickly began. It was her word against his. She had been thrown out of the school just hours before graduation.

Her relationship with Mark had ended painfully and abruptly too.

Her hands covering her face, she sobbed, her heart aching for the man she still loved. The man who couldn't, wouldn't, believe her side of the story over his childhood friend's accusation.

***

The blast of cool air from the refrigerator didn't do anything to quell the heat Mark felt burning inside him. Fired again. Again! He couldn't tell Joey, or he'd be out on his ass, homeless. Jackie's words kept ringing in his ears. *I'm sorry I have no choice left.* Truth was, she wasn't sorry. Applying for the King Mills Flour job had only gained her resentment and sealed his fate. Well, now, at least he had the possibility of that to fall back on. If he won the job.

He reached into the fridge and grabbed the nearest beer bottle. It didn't matter what kind it was today. His usual fussiness about the kind he drank had no hold on him this minute, this second. Not even closing the fridge door, he reached for the string attached to the adjacent cabinet handle that had a bottle opener on the end. The string was there but it slipped through his fingers. The opener was missing.

"Shit!" A jolt of nerves flared in his body. He needed to get this bottle open. Hurriedly, he ransacked all the kitchen drawers looking for the opener. It was gone. And there wasn't anything else in the house he could use. He paced the long narrow kitchen like a caged tiger.

"There's only one choice left." He grasped the bottle by its base and raised it over head, aiming the neck of the bottle for the edge of the porcelain sink.

The bottle struck the sink, shattering. Beer and broken glass spewed all over the now chipped sink edge, the kitchen cabinets, floor and on Mark. Pain seared his hand as blood dripped from where a shard of glass cut it, adding to the mess on the kitchen floor.

Wrapping a wad of paper towels around his hand, he surveyed the mess he'd made over want of a beer. Then he check his hand. A deep cut on his palm was going to need stitches. *What the fuck am I doing? Am I really so desperate for alcohol I'd do something so idiotic? Am I really that fucked up over it?* An image of his drunken father burned through his mind.

Leaving the disaster, he stomped off to the get his laptop. In minutes he was on the website.

CHAPTER TWENTY-TWO

Breaking from the memory and the sadness, Jackie pondered the situation. Without Mark, she would have to resume the bread baking duties, starting each morning at three. Bread baking would mean she couldn't help Isabelle with pastry duties. She would have to ask another staff member to help get them done before opening time at six. It wasn't going to be easy. In fact, it might be impossible to maintain the variety of offerings for the time being until Jamaica was ready to return.

Jamaica. Jackie knew Jamaica deserved a phone call about Mark and the situations that had been occurring. Until now, she had hoped to let them slide, handling them herself. But there was no way she could keep Jamaica in the dark anymore. She picked up her cell phone and dialed Jamaica's number.

"Hello," Jamaica answered, a crying baby in the background.

Jackie cringed. What did she think she was doing, burdening her boss with this bullshit? Jamaica had her hands full with a newborn. Well, not a newborn anymore, but close enough. Six weeks wasn't a long time. "Jamaica, it's Jackie."

"Yup, know that. I was going to call you. How's it going?" Jamaica asked before shushing her baby.

Feeling the sweat form under her armpits, Jackie took a deep breath and delved into the explanation. "Not as good as you might have hoped. Mark hasn't worked out. He made two major errors. I mean major. Then this morning, he attacked a customer. I had to let him go."

"What?" Jamaica cried, her voice loud and sharp. The baby, who had quieted down, started to cry again. "Attacked a customer? Was he out of his mind?"

"Pretty much." She went into detail about the flying pastries. "Mr. Stewart wasn't exactly blameless, but still. So, I fired Mark. I'll be picking up the bread baking duties again, and I'll work out some arrangements with Jenny and Vanessa to split the pastry duties."

"Wait, don't do that yet. I've been thinking about coming back part-time. Maybe now is the perfect excuse to do it. Ronnie can't say no."

Jackie's mind swirled with the idea. It was only six weeks. Was Jamaica really serious about returning to work so soon? "What about Willow?"

"I'll leave her with Ronnie. She'll sleep through the entire thing and never miss me. You won't believe it, but she's nearly sleeping through the entire night already. Talk about luck. Anyway, I'll come in at five tomorrow morning and give you a hand with the baking. Ronnie can watch her until seven. It's about time he took over the lead a little bit with his own daughter."

Jackie chewed her lower lip before asking, "Are you sure? I hate to take you away from her so soon."

"Nonsense. I've been going stir crazy away from the bakery. I'm feeling fine, and Willow is doing well. There's no reason why I can't return to work on a part-time basis. Besides, I need to talk to you about a new client order."

"New client?"

"Did you hear about the new microbrewery opening up in town at the end of the month?"

Jackie thought a few seconds. "I've heard about a new restaurant opening up soon. Maybe they are one and the same?"

"Could be. Anyway, this microbrewery is planning to open soon, and they want to buy all their bread items from us."

"Great. We could use another client."

"That's not all. They want us to supply them with a pretzel bun for their menu. I was going to set you to the task of developing the recipe."

Jackie's chest tightened. "Mark would have been great for that task. He's a master at breads."

"Well, it's on you now, girlfriend. So, get on it. We don't have a lot of time. We'll talk more about it tomorrow when I come in."

"Okay. We'll see you in the morning," Jackie said.

"Until tomorrow," Jamaica said. "And don't beat yourself up for firing Mark. If his transgressions deserved it—and I have perfect faith that you made the right call—then he deserved to be fired. I realize it's hard considering you two have more history than going to school together?"

Jackie sucked in a breath as the bottom fell out of her stomach. *How did she know that? How much did she know?* "Yeah." It was all she could think to admit. All she cared to admit at this point.

"I trust your judgment. I'll see you tomorrow."

Jackie hung up the phone just as Isabelle knocked on the office door jamb. "Your mother is here to see you."

CHAPTER TWENTY-THREE

Alwina Thorndike stood at the sales counter, her feet planted firmly to the spot.

Isabelle said, "She'll be right with you. She asks that you please have a seat and that you order anything you'd like, on her."

"Hmm. It should be. It's the least she can do for her mother." Alwina tapped her finger to her cheek as she scrutinized every pastry in the case and every bagel and bun on the shelf. "I'll have a lemonade and a cinnamon bun."

"Great." Isabelle smiled prettily. "I'll warm up the bun and bring everything over to your table."

As the woman walked away, Isabelle dropped the false smile. She had a hard time believing this unpleasant woman had given birth to Jackie. They weren't close friends, but Jackie was easy to work with and had stepped into Jamaica's role gracefully. Mark hadn't told her what this woman had said to Jackie on the phone a couple of weeks ago, only that she'd been rude and obnoxious to her own daughter. The reaction from Jackie on hearing her mother was here told Isabelle the visit would not be a pleasant one.

Swinging aside the kitchen doors, Jackie immediately spotted her mother across the room. Picking up a cup of coffee, she walked over and took a seat across from her as she sat enjoying her lemonade and bun. "Hello, Mother."

"It's about time."

"I'm on the clock, and so are you." Jackie set a kitchen timer on the tabletop. "I have bread in the oven. Consider yourself lucky I'm here talking to you at all."

Alwina sat back, a startled look on her face. "Is that any way to treat your mother?"

Jackie sighed and sat back in her chair. "What do you want?"

"I wanted to see your new workplace." Alwina glanced around before daintily placing a tidbit of bun in her mouth.

"No, you didn't. I've been working here well over a year, and suddenly you want to see what it looks like?" Jackie sat forward, almost hunched over the table. "What do you really want?"

She took a long leisurely sip of lemonade before answering. "My car broke down. I have some money to fix it, but it isn't enough. I need five hundred more."

"What is wrong with it?"

Crossing her arms over her chest, Jackie cocked an eyebrow and waited.

"If you must be so nosey, it needs a new radiator."

Biting her lip to prevent laughing at the irony of the moment, "My, my. It's a good thing I have a real job instead of just a man and a house full of kids. Otherwise, who would you beg money from?" Her voice was crisp and dripping with sarcasm, her arms still folded over her chest.

"Don't get fresh with me, missy. Just give me the money. If not, I'll go."

"Really? You'll go away if I turn you down?"

"What choice would I have?" Alwina stared back at her daughter across the white expanse of the tabletop.

"Sounds good to me."

Alwina placed a hand on her chest and pitched her voice loudly. "You won't help your own mother?"

Jackie's head whipped around. Fortunately, only Isabelle was in the shop. But still ... "I'll give you the money on one condition."

"Anything. What is it?"

Jackie stared her down. "You never contact me again."

Alwina looked aghast, then hurt, then angry. "But I'm your mother. You should be taking care of me."

"You stopped being my mother a long time ago." Jackie stood up. "Go see your eldest child if you need something. I wash my hands of you."

"But—"

"No buts. Accept the money and the condition or leave empty-handed."

Fury filled Alwina's face. "You're a good-for-nothing child. I should have listened to your father and aborted you when I had the chance."

The air sucked out of Jackie's universe in an instant. No words, no movements, even her heart stopped beating for a few seconds as the words sunk deep. Gasping for breath, she stood up. She walked through the kitchen doors and retrieved her checkbook. Silently, zombie-like, she wrote the check and delivered it to Alwina, holding it out to her.

When it was taken from her hand, Jackie spat, "Get out."

The woman snatched up her handbag and bolted out the shop door.

Head high and back stiff, Jackie returned to the locker room to grab her car keys. In the privacy of her car in the parking lot behind the building, she cried her last tears over her mother.

A darkness and loneliness crowded in on her in the small car. Opening the window didn't help. Her body ached from crying, but it also ached for something she couldn't quite put a finger on. She closed her eyes and tried to identify the feeling. Flashes of forest and the smell of pine came forward in her mind. And the firm but gentle masculine arms that had held her. The same ones that had held her in the locker room after her telephone conversation with her mother weeks ago. The ones that kept her safe. The ones that filled her with love and acceptance and understanding. They held her up, supported her like no one else did.

Jackie cried harder, realizing she had let those arms and that person go. Literally and figuratively. She had tossed him out of her life with no possibility of ever returning

CHAPTER TWENTY-FOUR

The twelve women sat together on one side of the room, taking up the first two rows of five chairs plus two additional in a third. Before them was the head table for officers, where Benjamin Salters sat, conferring with Jack Callahan and a few other men.

Jackie had never been inside the building. Old sepia pictures of men in military uniforms lined the walls. Walls of crumbling plaster and peeling paint evinced its age as did the scuffed linoleum worn through in spots. What curiosity she had, faded to sorrow for the inevitable loss of the greatest generation. Who would uphold the organization? Did they allow women these days or were they still strictly fraternal?

It was especially evident in front of the refreshment table. Jamaica had asked Jackie to bring a couple dozen chocolate chip cookies with her. It was her usual contribution to the meeting refreshments. Other women had brought snacks, but she had not seen a single man contribute to the refreshment table.

Mr. Salters banged his hand-carved wood gavel on the table, quieting the roar of the audience and sending people to their seats. After the usual report on the minutes of the last meeting and the treasurer's report, the floor was turned over for the election of officers.

As Regina and Jackie had discussed, one woman in the pack of women, stood and nominated another woman for an officer's position. She nominated Elowen Sparkle as treasurer, Vera August as secretary, Regina Maxwell as vice president. At each of the nominations, the company of twenty-three men had looked astounded.

After the nomination of Maddie Dailey for president, Jack Callahan had the audacity to suggest contesting the presidency wasn't necessary because Mr. Salters was doing such a fine job.

Madelaine Dailey had risen from her chair and replied, "Sir, every concern every woman in this room has ever brought before this organization has been ignored. We are tired of being ignored. If that means we must take over leadership of this organization to see our concerns heard and acted upon, then so be it. Besides, the by-laws of this organization demand an election for every officer."

The room of men had grumbled and whispered steadily throughout the voting process. Despite getting the word out to all the women business owners, the women attending were outnumbered. Without at least six male defectors, they were likely to lose.

After all ballots were filed and counted, the election coordinator rose to present the outcome. Warren Howard opened the tri-folded paper and said, "The results of the election stand as follows: treasurer is Michael Unger, secretary is Simon Poult, vice president is Jack Callahan, and president is Benjamin Salters. Congratulations to our officers."

"Congratulations, my ass," Vera August, the owner of Knit One! Grumbled before standing up, grabbing her empty plate from the refreshment table, and heading for the door.

All the remaining women did the same: standing up en masse, retrieving their goodie plates and leaving the meeting. Outside the VFW hall on the sidewalk they congregated, bitterly disappointed, but not totally surprised. "The Dockside Restaurant is expecting us, ladies," Maddie called out.

Walking beside Jackie, Regina said, "This could be a long night."

Maddie Dailey banged her beer bottle down on the tabletop. "Meeting adjourned until the second Monday in August, 7 pm here at The Dockside."

"Why didn't you run for secretary? I thought you wanted the position." Regina whispered to Jackie.

"Vera August will do a fine job. Besides, I'm only filling in for Jamaica. I'm not really a business owner."

"Weren't you listening? Our new Fulton River Business Women organization is going to allow any woman working in the business sector within the town limits to join. Not just owners. So, you could have taken the office."

Jackie leaned close and lowered her voice to a whisper. "I might not be working in Fulton River much longer if I'm lucky."

Regina sat back, silently mouthing, "OhmyGod!" Getting up to Jackie's ear, she whispered, "Where are you going?"

"I applied for my dream job. Fingers crossed." She held up both hands with two sets of crossed fingers on each.

Maddie came over to join them. "Well ladies, we got a lot accomplished tonight. Officers elected, by-laws drafted, and our next meeting set."

"Great job, Maddie," Jackie said. "What's the first topic on the agenda? The restrooms?"

"Definitely on the first agenda," Maddie replied, glancing at her watch.

Regina raised a finger. "I had an idea the other day. Perhaps we can get the town to designate the downtown area a women's entrepreneurial zone. Most of the shops are owned by women."

Jackie and Maddie looked shocked.

Maddie replied, "That's an awesome idea. You're right. I never thought of it that way. Most of the shops are owned by women. Tinker's Toys, Sparkle Jewelry, Bookworm's Paradise, Jam's, Rusch Art Gallery, Vera's knit shop."

"That's only half of them. How many are owned by men?" Jackie asked.

Regina raised an eyebrow. "Well, it's time to find out."

Jackie added, "Yeah, and how is it there were so many men in the Downtown Merchant Association?"

With stumped expressions, the three women looked at each other.

"Good question," Maddie replied, a twinkle in her eye and a devious smile on her face. "I think we need to take a closer look at their membership list."

CHAPTER TWENTY-FIVE

As Mark walked up the hallway to the baking classroom, he smelled the unmistakable scent of pretzels. Was that on tonight's lesson plan? Last week, Jackie had said the next class would be on Tart Tatin, a gooey apple tart baked upside down, then flipped right side up to serve, much like a pineapple upside down cake. Perhaps the agenda had changed for some reason. It would be just like Jackie to change the lesson plan without telling him.

Of course, she hadn't spoken with him since firing him from Jam Bakery. He wasn't even sure he still had the job of helping her with the baking class. He'd pondered that predicament for a while today, finally deciding to show up and see what happened. If he got the job at KMF, the more experience he had working with students, the better. Ten to one, Jackie was going to throw him out of class. But he was a betting man, so he'd take the risk and arrive as usual anyway. If she wanted him out, she was going to have to say so.

He rounded the doorway and stopped in his tracks. The closest set of kitchen counters was full of what looked like misshaped pretzels. Surrounding this was a mess of dirty bowls, wooden spoons, flour, and God only knows what else. Standing alongside the farthest counter was Jackie, slowly munching on a round pretzel.

"What the hell happened here?" he asked as soon as he could find his voice.

Jackie swallowed her last bite and said, "I've been working on a recipe."

"What for—round pretzels?" Mark cocked his head, his hands on his hips.

Pushing a stray strand of hair away from her face, Jackie said, "No, pretzel buns."

"Pretzel buns? What the hell for?"

As he inquired, he watched Jackie start to straighten out the counter, placing the dirty dishes and utensils in the sink for washing.

"None of your business," she said as she began washing the implements.

"Wait a minute." Mark walked over and stopped next to her. He stood very close to her, invading her personal space.

She started to back away, but he caught her arm. "Hold still a sec." He stared at her face for a few seconds. *She's just as beautiful as she was in pastry school. Maybe more so now with that air of confidence and the chip on her shoulder.*

Her eyes narrowed suspiciously the longer he did nothing. Then he reached out and swiped his finger down the bridge of her nose.

Jackie recoiled until she saw Mark's finger. It was covered with flour. "Um, thanks."

Leaning against the counter, her eyes narrowed on his bandaged hand. "What happened to your hand?"

"None of your business." Mark shot back.

"Fine." She went back to washing dishes.

Mark wiped the flour off on his jeans, then walked over to the counter and inspected the buns. There appeared to be three different sets of buns. He glanced over at Jackie. "Do you mind if I look at these?"

Calling over her shoulder, she said, "Knock yourself out."

He picked one bun up and tore it apart to see the inside. The first batch appeared to have burned slightly along the edges while the inside was still raw. The second batch also failed the same test, although it was more burned along the edges than the first. Mark moved on to the third batch. This batch looked better, with a nice chestnut brown coloring. When he tore it apart, the center was thoroughly cooked. But the texture was soft. It would not provide the chew expected from a pretzel bun. He turned back to Jackie. "I could help."

She set a freshly washed stainless-steel mixing bowl on a dishtowel before turning toward him. "If I wanted your help, I would have asked for it."

"Sorry, just offering," Mark said, his palms held up as he backed away from the counter.

Scowling, Jackie snarled, "What are you doing here?"

"Thought I'd come and help with class like I did last week, and the week before that, and etcetera." He steeled himself for the news. She didn't want him to help in class anymore.

"I would have thought you wouldn't come back after what happened at the bakery."

Mark rubbed his forehead. "Well, some people might not, but some people aren't me. I enjoy teaching or helping to teach as it is. So, can I continue?"

Jackie stood still for a moment, the wheels in her brain churning as far as Mark could tell. "I guess you can stay for tonight. I'll have to consider about next week."

"What's on the agenda for next week?" Mark asked. At Jackie's frown, he quickly added, "I'm just being curious."

She wiped her hands on the nearest dishcloth, "Charlottes."

Mark pictured the fancy looking ice-box cake similar to a trifle made by lining a springform pan with lady fingers and sponge cake and filling the interior with fruit puree and custard. It was a brilliant idea for a class project. Simple, elegant, and delicious. "You're really into these French desserts, aren't you?" He remembered her enthusiasm during that part of their program and how she'd assisted him with some of the finicky stuff.

Jackie gave Mark a shy smile. "There's nothing better than French pastries."

"What about Italian pastries? Or Danish? What's so good about the French?"

With one flip, Jackie threw the dishtowel over the back of the nearest chair. "Because that's where I spent so much time. In France or Montreal when I couldn't afford a flight across the pond."

Mark rubbed his chin between his index finger and thumb. "And for that reason, French pastries are the best."

Her arms crossed and her back rigid, she narrowed her eyes at him. "Yes."

"Just out of curiosity, what's your favorite?" Mark asked, leaning back against the counter.

"I'd have to say, créme brulée. I love the contrast between the crunchy burnt sugar topping and the creamy flan beneath."

"Hmm," Mark replied, liking the way her face lit up while describing the dessert.

Jackie gave Mark a curious look. "What would you say is your favorite dessert?"

"Me? Oh, I'm partial to an American invention called Boston cream pie," Mark said.

"Why's that?"

"Because it has three of the best things to come out of any kitchen: cake, custard, and chocolate ganache. What more can you want in a dessert?"

Before Jackie could reply, a few students walked into the classroom, signaling it was almost time for the start of class. She gave Mark a tentative smile and walked toward the front of the classroom to prepare for the demonstration.

Mark stayed where he was, leaning back against the counter, contemplating the conversation.

CHAPTER TWENTY-SIX

As happy as Jackie was to have her dear friend, back at the bakery, she was just as sad. Now that Jamaica was back doing the pastry work, Jackie was pushed back to bread baking duty. It wasn't that she didn't like bread baking. She did. It's just that she preferred pastry making. But that was also Jamaica's favorite, and the boss got to choose her work for herself and delegate the remainder. Jackie was also sad to be back on the 3 am shift. Coming in at 5 am to do the pastry work was a lot better for someone who really wasn't a morning person.

Her nerves were frayed about the pretzel bun issue. She still was not satisfied with her work on them. If Jamaica asked her about the buns, she was going to have to make her latest recipe and hope for the best.

Jamaica didn't waste any time on her first day back. After acknowledging the welcoming words of the staff and giving them updates about the baby, she set to work making the pastries like she'd never been gone. Jackie marveled at her tenacity while she went about the business of making the breads and rolls.

It was break time before Jackie knew it, and both she and Jamaica were taking a breather in Jamaica's office.

"I'm amazed at how quickly you've picked back up like you've never been gone a day," Jackie said, fingering her coffee mug.

Jamaica smiled. "Believe me when I say, I've been dreaming of this day for a few weeks." She took a sip of the steaming coffee in her cup before adding, "Don't get me wrong. I love my child. But there's a point when you want adult conversation and company. Not to mention something else to do besides change diapers, make bottles, and wash baby clothes."

Unable to relate, Jackie could only nod her agreement. "Still, it must have been nice to sleep later—no; scratch that. I don't suppose a newborn gave you much sleep."

Doubled over laughing, it was several minutes before Jamaica could talk. "No, sleep is a commodity I have yet to enjoy much of since Willow was born. Though she is getting better," she said, wiping the tears from her eyes.

Jackie grinned sheepishly. She didn't have much of a clue what it was like to have a newborn reliant on you. She had to hand it to Jamaica for continuing to work while caring for her infant.

Jamaica relaxed back in her office chair. She looked drained but content to be where she was, back at the helm. "Tell me what's been happening at the Downtown Merchant Association meetings."

"Well, us women banded together and presented our own slate of officers."

Snickering, Jamaica interrupted, "I bet that went over real well."

Jackie recounted the events that transpired up to and including the women leaving the meeting en masse to reconvene at The Dockside.

Her eyes closed; Jamaica had listened. "So, what came of it?

"The women formed their own group, Fulton River Business Women. By unanimous consent, it's open to any women engaged in business in the town of Fulton River, whether owner, manager, or staff. We meet at The Dockside second Monday each month at seven o'clock."

Jamaica's eyes popped open. "Really?" She sat up in her chair. "What about the DMA?"

"Business owners can belong to both, of course." Jackie's face brightened and she leaned forward. "You should have seen Madelaine at the last DMA meeting. She brought up the fact that some of the men in the room who counted themselves as members didn't fit the official membership requirement and should not be allowed to be there. *And* she questioned how many had been allowed to vote in the election. She suggested the election results be rescinded and the vote be held again."

Throwing back her head, Jamaica cackled loudly along with Jackie at the idea. When she caught her breath, "Oh, my God, I wish I had been there for that! Whoa! Leave it to Maddie to take on the DMA. She's fearless."

"She's out for blood and justice. She knows when she smells something rotten and she's going to root it out rather than cover it up or ignore it like a few of the women in the DMA. Snubbing her is something those men will live to regret."

"How is Kevin taking it?"

Jackie rubbed her cheek, then tapped her fingers against it. "He looked proud of her for standing up to that band of bullies. Even when the guys glared at him. I think they expected him to keep his wife in line."

Laughing again, Jamaica added, "Like that's ever going to happen. Well, bravo Kevin. He's a good man." She sat back, relaxed again. "What's the new group's first order of business?"

"Meeting with Mayor Marguerite D'Anguerra about the lack of public bathrooms in the park."

"Good. Much as I like the people using our bathrooms instead of leaving downtown altogether, the extra foot traffic isn't providing us any more significant sales numbers. And the crowds can get unruly at times. Waiting lines for our single bathrooms aren't very attractive to the dining customers either."

"Very true."

Jamaica started straightening up her desk top. "Anything else?"

"Yeah. Regina noted a majority of the business owners along downtown Main Street are women. We're also going to try to get this stretch of the street labeled a women's entrepreneurial zone."

"Great idea!" Jamaica rocked back in her chair and continued to rock gently. Jackie mused it must be a habit now with little Willow. "Regina Maxwell, she's one sharp cookie."

"Did I mention she's our Vice President?"

"No! That's great. Between her and Maddie, it will be a great start." Jamaica hesitated.

"Speaking of starts and finishes, can you continue with the adult ed class to the conclusion?"

Jackie's heart leapt in her chest. She had been dreading giving the class back to Jamaica. "No, that's fine. There's only one more left anyway."

The corners of Jamaica's mouth rose ever so slightly. "A little bird told me Mark has been helping you."

Her eyes on her hands in her lap, Jackie confessed. "Yeah. He wanted to help. And I gave him a chance. Fifteen students doesn't sound like a lot for one person but with hands-on stuff and verbal instructions, I appreciated his help."

Jamaica's smile broadened. "I heard you were a good team."

Should I tell her why Mark wanted to help? The self-serving bastard.

"You're blushing." Jamaica laughed.

"I was thinking of something else."

"Uh huh!" Jamaica winked.

Jackie went rigid. "No, Jamaica, really—"

She held up her hand, palm forward. "Look. No need to get defensive with me. It's your business and your love life."

"There's nothing—"

"Girlfriend, you are so busted you don't even realize it." Jamaica hefted herself out of the comfortable chair. "Last class tonight?"

"Yes, charlottes."

"Mark going to help?"

"I haven't asked him."

"Do it," Jamaica said with a wink.

"Oh, one more thing. I was in Regina's shop a little bit ago. She has some beautiful hanging plants I thought would look wonderful hanging in the front window of the bakery. She agrees it would give it a homey atmosphere. What do you think?" Her insides trembled a little waiting for an answer. It was an unusual request. Not strictly product quality or service oriented as had been her other suggestions.

Jamaica's mouth puckered up and her thumb and index finger played with her lower lip. "I guess we can get a couple and see how it looks. Would you take care of the selection and hanging?"

"Sure, though I'll ask Regina for some advice on the selection."

Jamaica's face turned serious. "How's that pretzel bun recipe coming along?"

Trying not to cringe, Jackie replied, "I've got a recipe that I think is pretty good. It's not what I would consider the best."

"You have to get that finalized. The pub is due to open next week. I don't want to lose this customer." Jamaica tapped the tabletop with her fingertip. "Make me a batch before you go home today. I want to taste what you've got so far."

"Okay." Jackie got up from the table and shuffled back to the locker room, where she kept the recipe card for the pretzel buns. This was not what she wanted to have happen today. But she could pull this off. She pasted a smile on her face as she walked back into the kitchen and set to work putting the dough together for its first rise.

Turning the bun over and over, Jamaica inspected the exterior of the fresh pretzel bun Jackie had delivered to her. The outside had the tawny color of a pretzel, and the surface had the shine. A few granules of salt clung to the glossy chestnut brown top. Taking a knife, she cut the bun down the middle, horizontally, separating the top from the bottom. She brought the bun to her nose and inhaled deeply. "Smells like a pretzel."

Jackie shifted her weight between her feet, her hands fisted at her sides. Deep worry lines etched her face as she watched Jamaica pinch the center of the inner surface of the top bun.

"The texture is springy." Ripping off a piece, she popped it into her mouth and rolled it around with her tongue. As Jackie watched, barely breathing, Jamaica tore a large piece from the top bun and tasted it.

Jamaica frowned. "It has an off-taste," she said, setting the bun down on the kitchen table in front of her. "I can't quite put my finger on the flavor, but something isn't right."

Jackie's shoulders slumped. She tried to remind herself Jamaica needed this client's business. She needed a great pretzel bun for them. Jamaica also knew this wasn't Jackie's forte. Unfortunately, it wasn't hers either.

"It's not right," Jamaica said to Jackie, disappointment lacing her tone. Feeling as though she were about to cry, Jackie wordlessly picked up the plate of buns sitting on the table and dumped them into the nearest garbage can. "I'll try again tomorrow."

Jackie sat in her car, wiping away her tears. It was nearly quitting time, and she had walked out for some fresh air and some privacy. Privacy for a good cry. Her heart heavy, she tried to think it through. *How am I going to get these damn buns right? The last thing I want is for the bakery to lose this client because of my failure.*

A little voice came out of nowhere in the back of her head reminding her that Mark was the master bread maker. Maybe he could figure out the pretzel bun project. Mark. It was too bad he was gone. He could have this figured out, probably quickly. *Well, he did offer to help me, and I turned him down, without so much as a thank you. Maybe I was too hasty?*

CHAPTER TWENTY-SEVEN

Given a thousand guesses as to who was calling him, Mark would never have thought Jackie the Thorn would be on the other end of the connection. He was so shocked he didn't even hear the words she was saying after he recognized her voice. So much so that she had to ask him if he was still on the cell phone.

"Yup, I'm here," he said, still shaking his head to clear the surprise from his brain in order to listen.

"What do you think?" Jackie said, impatience creeping into her voice.

Mark scratched his chin with his free hand as he held the cell phone to his ear with the other. "About what?"

"Mark, you didn't hear a word I said, did you?"

"Sorry Thornbush, can't say that I did."

"Don't call me that, or I'll forget the entire proposition."

"What proposition might that be," Mark said, running his fingers through his hair. This had to be good if Jackie was laying it on him by phone after firing him less than a week ago. And did she really think he'd come to her rescue, no matter what it was?

Forgetting for a moment that he might have deserved being fired for arguing with a customer, he believed he'd really pulled his weight at the bakery. Tried to help them out as best he could. Even tried to upgrade their offerings. How was he supposed to know the rolls were supposed to be coarse to hold up to the fillings? He'd done his best. Well, the cake fiasco. Okay, so maybe he'd fucked up a few times.

Still, he was a good guy, always on time, never burned a batch of anything. Maybe she's come to see that fact. Maybe Jackie was calling to hire him back?

"I need your help on a special project," Jackie said.

"Why me?" Mark said warily. There was something more to this that Jackie wasn't saying. He had to ferret it out of her.

"Well, for starters, you have the time and energy to do it. And you're good with breads."

"So —"

"So, if you aren't employed elsewhere yet, perhaps you could come back and help me develop this product for the bakery."

"What's the product?" Mark had a feeling he knew what it was, but he needed to hear her say it. In saying it, she would be admitting defeat.

"Pretzel buns."

Mark smiled into the phone. He was right. Jackie hadn't been able to work out a viable recipe for pretzel buns, and now here she was calling on him to save the day. "Pretzel buns, huh. I thought you were working on that. As I recall," Mark rubbed the stubble on his chin. "You didn't need my help. What changed your mind?"

"Yeah well, I am working on it. I can't quite work out an acceptable recipe. It's for a new client, so it's important."

"When do I have to let you know by?" Mark asked, tapping his free hand against the door of his truck.

"Now. I need to know immediately. If you can't or won't do it, I'll have to make other plans." He could hear the tension in her voice.

Mark ran a hand through his hair. To go or not to go. He'd love the opportunity to show Jackie how it was done correctly. He had every confidence he could figure out a working recipe for a good-tasting pretzel bun in a couple weeks. It would be worth doing it just to see the look on Jackie's face once he figured it out. "Okay. I'll help," he said. "By the way, how long do we have to do this?"

"Seven days." Jackie said. "Oh, one more thing. You're helping me has to remain a secret."

"So, who's paying me then?" There was no way he was going to do this for free.

"Me. It will be coming out of my pocket." She disconnected.

Staring at the phone in his hand, her answer didn't make him happy.

Being back at the bakery after closing time made it seem like he'd never left. This time, he didn't have any baking responsibilities. His participation was more as a consultant.

To explain her additional time at the bakery after hours, she was adding a new item to the bakery menu. The La Mange style baguette dough poolish had to be made the day before and required an overnight rise in the refrigerator.

Mark found it fascinating to watch Jackie in action. Something he hadn't had time to do before when they had worked together. There was a flow and grace to her movements that captured his attention and would not let it go. As he tried to work on the project, he often found himself watching Jackie put the simple mix of flour, yeast, and water together and knead it gently.

The project was simple as far as Mark was concerned. There were enough pretzel bun recipes online to peruse for ideas. All had nearly the same steps, and most had the same ingredients.

For their first test run, Mark chose a recipe that had universal ingredients and instructions. The outcome was not bad, but they were not satisfied with the sturdiness of the bun. Besides that, the bun itself came out more like a ball instead of a bun-shaped disk.

Another evening of web searching gave Mark a few more suggestions for the next day's experiments. Again, the bun wasn't sturdy enough to withstand a juicy burger and condiments, though pressing it into a flattened disk before dropping it into the baking soda water had solved the shape problem. The dough, when baked, had come out more like a hamburger bun.

This process went on for nearly a week. Each day, Mark came up with a new modified recipe which Jackie baked, and together they evaluated the results.

"It's still missing something," Mark said, his eyes closed as he concentrated on the tastes in his mouth.

Jackie popped another small bit in her mouth. "I think we need to add the light brown sugar back into the dough. The taste alteration it gives is subtle, but it makes a difference."

Mark surveyed her face. "Well, it's your project. If you feel it's right. Personally, I'd leave it alone."

"I have to make the batch for the client and the chef tomorrow."

"Like I said, it's your project." He shrugged. "And your head."

***

Friday, their deadline, Jackie made a batch that she and Jamaica could take to the restaurant's owner and chef. They sat at the restaurant's bar and waited while the chef made up a batch of burgers. The women looked at each other, each silently praying the consensus would be acceptance, as the chef came through the kitchen's door with a platter full of burgers encased in pretzel buns.

Her body trembled as the platter came closer and closer. "I can't handle this. I'll be waiting at the bakery for the verdict." Jackie bolted for the door.

CHAPTER TWENTY-EIGHT

Mark waited at O'Toole's Tavern for a message from Jackie about the buns. But his head was stuck thinking about that day eight years ago. It still continued to perplex him. If there was one thing Mark knew, what happened that day was totally out of her character. It just didn't make sense that she would take his sourdough starter without asking first. That's not the type of person she was.

He perfectly understood her reasoning for doing what she did. It was the final. The last exam for the entire program. Without an eatable sourdough starter, she would never have graduated. He'd have done the same thing in her shoes. But he would have asked her first. And he knew she would have given him half her starter without question. Just as he would have if she had asked him.

Mark sighed before tipping back his bottle. But it was empty. He started to gesture for another but caught himself and stopped. *One drink a day, man. You've met your quota.* Pat O'Toole walked over anyway after noticing his body language.

"Another?" He asked, removing the empty beer bottle.

"No, water please."

Pat did a double take. "Water?" He cocked his head as if perhaps he must not have heard the "Scotch and..." part of Mark's sentence.

"Yes, just water, with ice. Please." Mark frowned, an uneasy feeling in his chest. More than anything he wanted another beer. Another cold, frothy, hoppy lager. All it would take is a word to Pat. Mark fisted his hands together in his lap and mashed his lips together. *Shit. Don't do it.*

"Never mind, give me a non-alcoholic beer." Instantly he loathed himself. Loathed his lack of will power, resolve, whatever it was called. Maybe the non-alcoholic stuff wouldn't taste too bad.

Pat brought over the bottle. The questioning look on the bartender's face raised his ire. As did the returning train of his thoughts. He knew he held a boatload of resentment toward what Jackie had done. Everything in his life had been smooth sailing until that day. It was like a tsunami came and upended his life in one giant wave of disaster. One mistake on her part, and her huge coverup lie about it had ended the best period of his life. His life that had included her.

And still, eight years later, she continued to insist the starter was freely given to her. That she would not just confess the truth, that she was caught in the act by Paul, he could forgive her. But her lying and her continued lack of remorse at lying was the final straw.

"Hey, Mark, what are you doing here?"

Mark looked up from his cell phone to find Paul Drexell approaching. His eyes widened with amazement. "Hey Paul, never mind me, what are you doing in Fulton River?"

Paul signaled the bartender, pointed at Mark's non-alcoholic beer bottle, and flashed two fingers. "I'm an investor in a new microbrewery opening in town in a few days. I came to check the progress."

"Dudley Brew Works?"

"That's the one." Paul fished out his money clip and dropped a fifty on the bar top when Pat returned with the bottles. "Keep the change." He turned his attention back to Mark. "So, what are you doing in Fulton River?"

"I was helping an old friend develop pretzel buns for your new pub."

"You work at the bakery?"

"I used to. Now I'm a consultant. I was helping Jackie Thorndike with the recipe. You remember her, right?" Mark said slyly, toying with his bottle.

"How could I forget the Thorn." Paul laughed. "Is she still pissed at me for getting her thrown out of school?"

Mark's gullet seized, causing him to choke on the swallow halfway down his throat. When he stopped coughing, he set the bottle down on the tabletop hard. "You mean, it's true?"

"What's true? That I set her up?" Paul started chuckling again, his eyes gleaming, a knowing smile on his face. "You bet I did. We had to get rid of her so you could graduate first in the program, pal." He slapped Mark on the back before returning to his brew.

Grinding his teeth, trying to control his fury, Mark entwined his hands together on the bar top before him. "Paul—did you also contaminate her sourdough starter?"

Throwing back his head, Paul gave a hearty laugh. "Of course. It was a spectacular plan." He put his arm around Mark's shoulder and got close to his ear. "I knew her schedule. I knew when she was most likely to check and feed the culture, so it was easy to show up at the same time after I had contaminated it the day before. It was brilliant. She never even noticed the jar I gave her; the jar she took fresh starter from was yours."

Shrugging away Paul's arm, Mark added, "And when I noticed half my starter was missing, you said you saw Jackie take it." He stared at his hands, trying to keep them under control. Trying to keep them from breaking Paul's slimy neck.

"I did see Jackie take it. I didn't lie about that, pal."

Mark's gut lurched to a simmering boil. "You just omitted the part about offering it to her. And then lied to the investigation team when they asked you about the incident."

Paul grinned ear-to-ear. "It did the trick. You became numero uno overnight."

Standing, unable to tolerate the self-righteous bastard any longer, Mark started to walk away before he did something that might land him in jail.

"Hey, you're not sore about that, are you? I know you two were getting it on, but she was just another piece of ass, right?"

Mark whirled around and sprang back to the bar. Grabbing Paul by the arm, he twisted it behind the man's back. "I can't believe all these years I wasted trusting your word instead of hers."

"Let me go! How was I supposed to know you'd be so angry?" Paul's eyes flashed with fear, his face pale and clammy. "I thought you two had a rivalry going on?"

"We did. But it was a rivalry that spurred us on to work harder. Not to work against each other. Neither of us really cared who was first and who was second. We only wanted to graduate. And you stole that from her." With one hard stare, Mark flung Paul's arm away from him and strode for the door.

Sitting in his truck, Mark's swirling thoughts were interrupted by his ringing phone. He dragged it out of his pocket with the intent of checking the caller ID, but once he saw who the call was from, he answered immediately.

"Hello, Mark here," he answered.

"Mark, it's Frank Goss from King Mills Flour Company."

"Yes, sir, what can I do for you."

"I'd like to know if you'd still like the job here."

Mark didn't need to think about it. "Yes, I'd love it."

"It's all yours. Congratulations."

"Thank you, sir."

"Perhaps you could call early next week to discuss your starting date."

"That would be fine, sir; I'll do that."

"Great, we'll talk to you then," Mr. Goss said before disconnecting the call.

Mark walked back into the bar quickly, his cell phone in his hand.

"Everything okay?" Pat, the bartender, asked, one eyebrow raised.

"Yes, fine," Mark said, his heart not nearly as light as he thought it would be with such news. As he sat there stewing over the situation and the details Paul had revealed, Mark had a sinking sensation in his chest. Jackie had been telling the truth. Every word of the truth for eight years. No wonder she didn't trust him. Paul and he had stolen her graduation. And while she had been able to pull together a successful career so far, it still wasn't what she wanted. Her dream hadn't materialized. How much of her future was impacted and would be forever due to the terrible, diabolical farce Paul had played on her?

He looked at the phone still in his hand, overwhelmed with a heaviness in his chest and a thickness in his throat. Wasn't he doing exactly the same thing to Jackie as Paul did? Stealing her future? Stealing her dream?

CHAPTER TWENTY-NINE

Jackie disconnected the call and dropped the cell phone on the kitchen table. She buried her face in her hands. Tears flooded her eyes though she tried to stop them. Wiping them away with the palms of her hands, she looked around to see if anyone had noticed.

The KMF job was offered to someone else. Though she'd been "runner-up," according to Mr. Goss, their first choice had accepted the position. Jackie felt the burn in her chest as she contemplated the lost opportunity. Here she was, twenty-eight, stuck in a dead-end job. Sure, she loved working for Jamaica, and she loved Jam Bakery. But she'd been doing baking jobs now for eight years. It was time to move up somehow in responsibility. There was no way she could possibly own her own bakery. The KMF job had been a bright opportunity, complete with benefits like insurance and pension. Baking and teaching. It would have been a perfect fit.

After taking a swig from her cold coffee, Jackie got up from the kitchen table and headed for the locker room. She was stopped in her tracks by the return of Jamaica from the restaurant.

"We did it!" Jamaica announced as she walked through the kitchen.

Jackie's mouth dropped open.

"The buns were accepted," Jamaica added before flopping down on the kitchen chair.

"Great. I'm so relieved," Jackie said flatly.

Jamaica stopped short, the smile dropping from her face. "What's wrong?"

"Nothing. Nothing at all," Jackie replied.

"It doesn't sound like nothing," Jamaica said, her eyes narrowing on Jackie as if trying to see into her soul for the answer. "You worked hard on that recipe. I'm proud of you."

Her eyes were spilling tears and her heart breaking. "Mark did it."

"What do you mean, Mark did it?" Jamaica said, sitting up straighter in her chair.

"I asked Mark to help me with the recipe. He's been here every afternoon and evening for a week, long after everyone leaves, helping me figure out what to do to make the recipe better." She wiped her eyes with the heel of her hands. "He deserves the credit for this win. Not me."

"I'm sure it was a collaborative effort, Jackie." Jamaica gently rubbed her employee's shoulder. "You're a very talented baker. Between the two of you, it's no wonder the buns were a success."

Jackie cried harder. She held up her index finger before running off into the locker room. Returning in under a minute she handed Jamaica a manila envelope.

Jamaica's eyebrows knitted together. "What's this?"

"Mark had a suggestion about a new menu line of sprouted bread. I told him to do a market analysis if he believed it was a worthwhile project. So, he did."

"Didn't you talk to me about this very subject during your initial job interview?"

Jackie's breath and her tears seized up at the memory. It came seeping back to her. Their conversation had been lengthy that day, and they had discussed so many things. Had they really talked about this very subject? "We may have. I don't quite remember talking to you about it, but I do remember thinking about it a lot when I first was hired. Then forgot all about it with the bustle of the wedding reception food preparations and the wedding cake."

"I believe we did. So, Mark thinks it's a good idea too. I'll have a look at the analysis and let you know." Jamaica smiled and patted Jackie's shoulder again. "I like the idea."

CHAPTER THIRTY

Mark took a pull on his non-alcoholic beer bottle. It wasn't as great as a real beer but the crisp hoppiness of the brew satisfied his taste buds enough. The cold liquid slid down his throat, chilling his esophagus as it went down, giving him a slight pain in the center of his chest. The ache made him think of Jackie for some reason he couldn't quite understand.

Her reaction to his solving the pretzel bun problem should not have been a surprise. With a terse thank you, she'd sent a text saying they'd got the contract. He frowned, thinking about it. Not that he expected her to be happy. It had long been clear she wasn't in his corner, didn't have his back. And yet, he couldn't help feeling ... perturbed? No, that wasn't it. He couldn't help feeling sorry. Sorry that they didn't get along as well as they might have. As well as they should have.

From the day they first met back in culinary school, she'd caught his eye and intrigued him. With her brown hair pulled back from her face in braids, no makeup, and bright, sharp eyes, she was different from all the other women. There was intelligence in those eyes and a no-nonsense look in them that never wavered during classes.

After class, when the gang of them went out to the local watering hole for adult beverages, she was warm and engaging. Quick to laugh, loved to listen to music and the more experienced classmates' stories of baking disasters. She even told of turning her first batch of crème anglaise green by cooking it in an aluminum pot.

But the story that stole his heart was of her efforts as a young girl, trying to cook and bake to help out her single mom. How she was berated for every flaw in the food she had ready when her mother got home from work. She described crying herself to sleep, praying for someone to teach her how to cook, so her mother didn't have to rely on boxed mac and cheese and peanut butter sandwiches all the time.

After she shared that story with him, his heart was taken, swept up in her big brown eyes, the elegant curve of her neck, the sweep of her hair into a bun, and her excellent intentions that had been so ungraciously condemned. And despite how her mother treated her as a child, whenever her mother contacted her, almost always looking for money, Jackie didn't hesitate to give it to her. Even when it meant she'd be short of cash for food.

The ringing of his cell phone cut his thoughts off. The number was not identified but looked familiar, so Mark took the call. "Hello, Mark speaking."

"Mark, it's Frank Goss at King Mills Flour. How are you today?"

Mark sat up straight and set his bottle down on the table beside him. "Hello, I'm fine thanks. And yourself?"

"Good, thanks. Mark, I'm calling about the job. You hadn't called back about a start date. Have you changed your mind? It's yours if you're still interested in it."

Unable to breathe for a few seconds, Mark repositioned the phone. "Yes, I am still interested."

A vision of Jackie's face came to the forefront of his mind. She would be devastated by the news that he'd gotten the job. After watching her teaching her baking classes, Mark was sure she would be the better person for the job. Much as he wanted it and had the same amount of experience, he had felt, all along, that she was the better candidate for the position. "Just for my own information, would you tell me who the runner-up was?" Mark heard himself ask Frank.

"Ah, I guess I can tell you, it was your co-worker, Jackie Thorndike. It was a tough decision, but I think we've made the right choice. You both have the same level of teaching experience, but you have the better credentials. You graduated from the culinary institute program. She did not."

Mark mulled over the information for a few seconds. He was first, Jackie was second. Because she'd been screwed over in culinary school and he'd ridden her coattails in the adult baking classes.

Suddenly the position had lost its luster. He wasn't sure he really wanted it. Wasn't sure he'd ever really wanted it in the first place. Perhaps he'd only applied out of spite, just to be a thorn in Jackie's side for a change. He had known she was going for the job, and it seemed like a challenge—a personal challenge to him. One he couldn't refuse. And more to the point, it became clear that he considered himself lucky no matter which way it turned out. If he got the job, he was lucky. And if he didn't, he would keep the bread baking job at Jam Bakery. That was until he got fired.

Jam Bakery. Mark's heart gave a lurch. He'd missed the place when he was fired. Missed running the breads division of the bakery. It was like running his own business in a way. And having the pretzel bun project had been a godsend to getting him back into the fold again.

"Hello? Mark?" Frank Goss said over the phone line.

Mark snapped to attention. "Yes, Mr. Goss. Can I get back to you about accepting the position in, say, a day or two?" He picked up his bottle and took a quick sip.

"Is there a problem, Mark?"

"No, I don't think so. I just want to be sure before I say yes. It's a big career change."

"We could really use your milling skills here at KMF. Your time at Elsmore Bread Company in Maine would be invaluable to our baking school." When Mark didn't reply, Frank Goss sighed. "I'll expect to hear back from you in two days with an answer. And please be sure to call this time."

"You got it," Mark said before disconnecting the call.

He took a deep pull on the brew and swallowed the mouthful slowly. If he could maneuver it just right, he could get what he wanted while still giving Jackie what she wanted as well.

He picked up the phone and dialed Jamaica's number. "Jamaica, it's Mark Zutka. I have a proposition for you."

CHAPTER THIRTY-ONE

Kicking back at home, relaxing for a change, Jackie sipped her wine. Having to put up with Mark again while he worked on the project was bad enough. But then, to imagine him gloating over his success wasn't good for her teeth-grinding habit. She had tried to concentrate on her own work. More than twice, she'd caught herself making major mistakes during the dough-making process. They had been easy enough to fix. But it still irked her that she'd been distracted enough to make them in the first place.

Even her last baking class hadn't gone very well this past week. She didn't have enough hands to help all the students at the same time. One student had packed up her supplies and left in exasperation. Mark's loss had definitely been felt.

It had been a tough week, but it was almost over. Tomorrow was Friday, then she'd have two days to herself. Jackie laid her head back on the chaise lounge chair, closing her eyes. The late afternoon sun beat hot on her eyelids as she tried to relax. As she contemplated getting a hat or a pair of sunglasses, her cell phone rang.

"Hello Miss Thorndike, it's Frank Goss at King Mills Flour. How are you today?" a familiar voice said over the phone.

Jackie sat up straighter and set the glass of wine down. "I'm fine sir, how are you?"

"Good, good. I'm calling about the job you interviewed for a few weeks ago."

"Yes, sir." Jackie stood up from the chair and began to pace the small wood deck.

"Our top candidate has suddenly declined the job offer, leaving us free to offer it to you, the runner-up."

Jackie stopped pacing and thought. The lead candidate turned down the job? Whatever for?

"Mr. Goss, do you know why the top candidate refused the position, and would you be willing to share that information with me?" Jackie held her breath.

"He declined because he had a better offer elsewhere," Mr. Goss explained.

"Really?" Jackie could hardly believe someone would go through the interviewing process then find something better than King Mills Flour Company to work for.

"So he said," Frank Goss added.

"He. It was a man," Jackie's mind clamped onto that fact for some reason and wouldn't let go.

"Yes. He declined the position. Said he was happy with the job he had."

It can't be Mark. Mark was out of a job. So it couldn't be Mark. For an instant, Jackie felt bad for Mark—knowing he really needed the job and was immediately available for it. Then her own elation caught up with her. She had the job she wanted, had prayed for, for all these weeks. She was finally going to be able to teach baking as a career.

"Hello? Miss Thorndike?" Mr. Goss asked, "Are you still there?"

"Yes, and I'm thrilled to get the job, but can you give me a day? I can call you tomorrow," she said before he could change his mind. "I only want to give notice here. Then I'll be free to say yes."

After cleaning up her workspace the next day, Jackie approached Jamaica. "Can you spare me a few minutes this morning?"

Giving her a sidelong glance, Jamaica replied, "Of course. Meet me in my office in half an hour?"

With a nod, Jackie said, "I'll be there," wringing her hands on her apron before heading for the locker room. Half way there, Jamaica called her back.

"Oh! Did you hear the news? Senator Perrot's daughter, Caroline, is getting married. We should make a pitch to get the catering contract or at least the cake. It's probably going to be a huge event."

Stunned, Jackie didn't know what to say. She would be leaving the bakery. But she didn't want to spring the news right this instant. Fumbling for something to say, she blurted out, "Are they going to get married here in Fulton River at their summer house or back in some swanky place in Montpelier where they live?"

"Don't know yet. I only know the groom is David Hayes Wescott."

Jackie whistled at the name. "Independently wealthy Wescott? Wow! Talk about a power wedding!"

Jamaica nodded eagerly, "I know. Think what a feather that would be in our cap."

"They're probably going to go full hog, five or eight course meal. We can't do that."

"True. That would be out of our league. But we could get the cake."

Jackie murmured before walking away. "Yeah." Her mind racing with the possibilities while her heart sank knowing she would not be here to craft it even if Jamaica managed to win that contract.

As she changed into street clothes, Jackie shook off the wedding idea and practiced various versions of her pronouncement. Done dressing early, she sat down on the wooden bench and stared at her visage in the mirror as she practiced until it was time to meet Jamaica. She knocked on the office door and paused.

"Come on in," Jamaica said, gesturing toward a chair opposite her at the large white, wooden desk.

"Thanks." Jackie settled into the stiff ladderback chair.

Jamaica looked at her earnestly, a light smile on her lips and a twinkle in her eye. "So, what can I do for you?"

Setting a hand on each knee, Jackie leaned forward slightly. "I, um, just wanted to, um tell you ..." Jackie swore under her breath before continuing. This was harder than she thought it would be. She'd only worked for Jamaica for a little more than a year and a half, but it was still one of the best places she had worked. Giving it up was harder than she thought it would be, even for her dream job.

Jamaica shifted in her chair. "What did you want to tell me?"

Jackie looked down at her hands, still clasped to her knees, and took a deep breath. "I wanted to let you know, I've, um, been offered another job, and I'm going to accept it." She waited for the horror to strike Jamaica's eyes, to see her adverse reaction. But none came.

Instead, Jamaica continued to smile. And her eyes widened but still twinkled as if in—was it merriment? "Congratulations," Jamaica said, shocking Jackie.

It was almost as if Jamaica knew it was going to happen. As if she knew Jackie was going to be giving her notice. But how could she? Jackie had never said anything to her about applying for the job at KMF. Then a thought zipped through Jackie's brain. Maybe Mark had said something about her interviewing for the job. Maybe he had told Jamaica out of spite? Worried that Jamaica might have known, Jackie blurted out, "You act as though you've known I was going to give my notice."

A wide grin split Jamaica's face. "I cannot tell a lie. I've been waiting for you to tell me."

Jackie's eyes widened as Jamaica told her this. "You mean you knew I was going to get the job?"

Jamaica nodded enthusiastically.

Stammering, Jackie asked, "How did you know? I only just found out yesterday. Did they contact you for a reference?"

"No. Mark told me."

Jackie swore, her gut filled with fury at the betrayal. She got up from the chair and began pacing the small office.

Holding up her right hand, Jamaica said, "Wait a minute. Let me explain. It's not what you think." Once again, Jamaica gestured to the chair she had been sitting in. Reluctantly, Jackie resumed her seat.

Jamaica continued. "Mark came to me a few days ago with a dilemma. He really wanted his bread baking job back here at Jam

Bakery. But he'd been offered the teaching job at KMF, which he really didn't want."

Jackie's eyebrows rose, and her eyes widened again. Mark had been offered the KMF job before her. How is it that she'd been offered the same job?

"I know what you're thinking. Mark inquired who the runner-up for the job was, and he found out it was you. So he had an idea. He came to me and offered to let you have the KMF job if I would let him take your bread baking position."

Unable to move, Jackie sat and processed the information before speaking. "He really wanted my bread baking job?"

"Yes."

A lump formed in Jackie's throat at the thought of the arrangement. "And he turned down the teaching job to let me have it?"

"Well, yes."

Jackie rubbed her forehead with the palm of her hand. "And you agreed to this?"

She shrugged. "I like to see people happy. He promised no more shenanigans." Jamaica sat back in her chair and beamed. "I know you've wanted to do the pastry work here since the day you were hired. That's the whole reason you left Chang's in Boston. You expected to do pastry someday. I think we even discussed it. You've enjoyed every second I was gone on maternity leave so you could help Isabelle bake pastries to your heart's content. Don't think I don't know you spent a lot of morning time making pastries," Jamaica raised her eyebrows. "I also know how much you enjoyed teaching the adult-ed baking class. And I hear you're darn good at teaching baking. It doesn't take a rocket scientist to figure out you'd take the KMF job if given the opportunity."

"Oh, and two last things. I know you gave all the credit to Mark for the pretzel bun recipe. Mark told me you figured out the final recipe for the buns. Adding the light brown sugar made it perfect."

Sitting quietly for a few seconds, Jackie's head spun with the implications. Mark hadn't thrown her under the bus. She was set up. Set up to win the job she wanted so badly. She should be furious with Jamaica and Mark for plotting her future. But she couldn't. "I guess I had better call Frank Goss and officially accept the position. But what was the second thing?"

"I've studied the market analysis and done a little of my own research. The sprouted bread line is a go. And I thank both you and Mark for the incentive."

Smiling, Jamaica stood up and started to leave the office. "Call Mr. Goff. Use my office. And don't come out until you've done the deed," she closed the door behind her.

Shaking her head in disbelief, her fingers trembling, Jackie dialed Frank Goss's number.

CHAPTER THIRTY-TWO

Coming from the bright sunlight into the darkness of O'Toole's Tavern, Jackie couldn't see anything at first. As her eyes adjusted to the lack of light, she could make out more features: the pool table, the booths along the walls, the tables littering the middle of the floor. Across the room, she spotted the bar and tried to make out the shapes of the people sitting there. Did any of them look like Mark? She wasn't sure.

Still trying to focus, Jackie walked toward the bar, identifying a few of the people as she got closer. Rudy Hayes, the mechanic at Gas & Go; Wendall Sprit from the hardware store; and Malcolm Edams, the insurance agent down on Main Street, all sat huddled together sipping at their beers, conversing. Down at the opposite end of the bar sat a lone figure, shoulders hunched, head hanging down as if contemplating the pink contents of his soda glass. Or was he asleep? Either way, he was in for some company, like it or not.

Slipping onto the barstool beside his, she signaled Pat, the bartender, for a beer and then looked over at the man she had come to see.

Mark's eyes had locked on her when she sat down, and he silently observed her. Jackie glanced over her right shoulder to look at him. "Hi," she said.

He took a sip from his glass before answering. "Hello."

Pat placed the mug of ale before Jackie and walked away. She took a sip of the cold brew. The frozen mug dripped condensate onto the bar top, soaking the slim paper cocktail napkin Pat had placed under it. "So, I guess I should thank you."

Mark sat up a little straighter on his barstool. "Don't thank me, thank Jamaica. She made it all happen."

Jackie sat silent for a moment, eying the tiny bubbles rising in her beer mug. "Why? Why did you turn down the teaching job? I thought that's what you wanted."

Turning on his barstool to face her, Mark said, "I thought so too at first. When I applied for the job, I wanted it bad. Who wouldn't? Easy hours, no weekends or holidays, full benefits."

Cocking her head to the side, Jackie asked, "So what changed your mind?"

Mark drained the last of his glass and set it down. "Helping you during your baking class. I'm not saying I didn't enjoy it, but I saw what you went through to prepare for the lessons and then what you went through dealing with all those people. It was tough. I decided I'm not cut out for that. Dealing with people. Plus, there was the pretzel bun project."

"What about it?"

Mark signaled Pat for another by holding up his empty glass. "Working on that project was fun. It caught my attention. Gave me a challenge. When it was finished, there was such a sense of accomplishment. I knew then that baking is what I really wanted to do. I wanted to continue to bake, and if I could get the bread baking job back at Jam, I'd be a happy man."

Jackie sipped at her beer then said, "But the hours?"

Frowning, Mark took the new drink from the bartender. "Yeah, I know. Sucky hours, and weekends and holidays sometimes. But it's me. Bread baking is me. I had to go with my gut feeling. Once I'd decided that it was just a matter of talking to Jamaica."

Looking at him with tears in her eyes, Jackie could only say, "Thank you."

"It's a win-win situation. You got the job you wanted, and I got the job I wanted."

"Still, thank you." She placed her hand on his forearm. "I really mean it."

Mark took Jackie's hand and cupped it between his own hands. "Besides, I'm hoping this can give us a new start."

Stunned, Jackie didn't know what to say. She could only stare into Mark's dark brown eyes. They were soft and warm and full of love.

"Wait. What about our feud? Did that change?"

Mark took her other hand in his. "As a matter of fact, it did."

She reveled in the warmth of his fingers against her cold hands. "I don't understand. When, and how did this happen?"

"I ran into Paul Drexell the other day. He told me the truth. He set you up to be caught so you would get thrown out of the program. Did you know that?"

Jackie's heart hammered in her chest. "I've always suspected it but could never prove it. Paul was always against me because we were dating. And I thought it odd that day when I left the room that he replaced the jar on the shelf without feeding it."

"Yup. He wanted you out. He deliberately gave you my jar and left it for me to find. You know the rest of the story."

"What was his motive?" She wrapped her arms around her middle and squeezed.

"So I could graduate as the top student in the program. Paul always had some sick kind of infatuation with me. He was always doing things to please me during junior and senior high school. I don't know why. He seemed to think he needed to win my friendship."

"What did he do?"

Mark frowned as he worked to remember. "Like when we were in junior high, he'd steal cigarettes from his father and bring them to me as a gift."

"A gift?"

"Yeah. Weird. He never smoked them. He'd give them to me and then sit there and watch me smoke them with a kind of creepy smile on his face." Mark shrugged. "If it wasn't cigarettes, it was alcohol or porn or even money sometimes."

"Very weird."

"I was hoping to put a lot of distance between him and me after graduation, but he heard where I was going and applied too. Like he had some kind of separation anxiety." Signaling Pat for another, he continued. "Before you and I got together, he hung around me all the time, which sucked. I started dating a lot of women just to get away from him."

"You did have quite the reputation as a ladies' man." Jackie chuckled. "Did it work?"

"Yeah, for a short time. But then he got more desperate. More clingy."

Jackie reflected a moment, twirling her bottle round and round. "Do you think maybe he's gay?"

"I don't know. He never made any kind of sexual advance. But he didn't like all those women, and he certainly didn't like it when you and I stayed together."

Shuddering, Jackie replied, "He made his dislike for me very clear from the beginning, which was why I was so surprised when he offered the starter. I thought it odd, but frankly, I was so worked up about the situation, I didn't look that gift horse in the mouth."

"I have one lingering question. Why didn't you tell me about this, about what Paul did before it blew up?"

Jackie shook her head. "Paul told me not to tell anyone, not even you. I thought at the time it was going to be a secret between the two of us." Her face crumpled a little as he watched. "Little did I know he was setting me up, had set me up."

"I'm sorry. I'm sorry his obsession with me got you thrown out of the program." Mark clasped her hands in his again. "I admit I was wrong to accuse you of stealing my starter. I know now it was given to you for devious reasons. I hope you can forgive me."

"Also" He eyed his pink drink before he set down his glass. "I want you to know I looked up the website we talked about." He glanced around, hoping no one else was listening to the conversation as it veered off on a tangent. "By the way, I'm drinking cranberry juice & seltzer."

"I was wondering what the heck that was." She chuckled then her face went serious again. "Do you mean that double A site I told you about?" Her eyes widened.

He nodded. "I was reading this online pamphlet called "Is AA for You?" and took a quiz to help assess my relationship with, you know."

"What did you learn?"

"I only had two out the twelve. They consider four sort of an action level."

"So, you're better off than you thought." Jackie's hand grasped his and squeeze, while her smile squeezed his heart.

"I guess so. It was a relief, to be sure. But I'm going to try a meeting. I don't want to keep sliding down that path of destruction."

Leaning over, Jackie kissed his cheek. "I'm proud of you. And I'll go with you if you want me to."

"Thanks, but no. This is something I have to do for myself, by myself." Mark took another sip of his spritzer before continuing.

She nodded her understanding, remaining silent.

"I had an idea last night. Maybe together, we can get the culinary school to reinstate you for the final project, and you can graduate."

Jackie's grip nearly crushed Mark's hand. "OhmyGod. That would be, oh, I can't tell you how happy that would make me." She bounced on her barstool.

"Easy girl, you're going to make people think I'm getting a lap dance or something." Mark laughed. "One more thing, I would like us to try to resume our previous relationship."

The guy who called her "The Thorn" was now telling her he'd like to be more than friends? It didn't make sense. And yet, there was a tingle as deep as her toes at the very thought of it. And were those butterflies in her stomach? *I must be losing my mind,* she thought as she tried not to smile.

"What's so funny?" Mark asked warily.

"Us."

Mark turned back to his drink, dropping her hand. He took a sip before adding, "Why do you say that?"

Jackie turned back to her own bottle and twirled it slowly between her hands. "It's been like seven, eight years since we've been together." The butterflies in her stomach swarmed. "Well, except for a month or so ago."

Mark winked. "We have some serious catching up to do."

EPILOGUE

Flames flared as Mark flipped the steaks on the patio's gas grill. It was a warm September night, perhaps the last before autumn officially began. He and Jackie had decided to celebrate with a couple of rib-eyes on the barbecue.

It had been a busy, exhausting afternoon moving Mark in after a day of baking work for him and teaching for Jackie. Not that Mark had a lot of stuff to move. It was more a matter of interspersing his things with Jackie's things in her apartment. Trying to figure out what to keep and what to store had taken them most of the afternoon. The diplomacy had been difficult at times, but in the end, they had managed to put together something that reflected both their personalities.

"Jack, I need a plate," Mark said as he checked the steaks.

From within the apartment, Jackie called out, "Coming." As she walked out through the open patio doors, carrying a platter, he turned off the grill.

He set the steaks on the platter, and they entered the kitchen. Setting aside the platter to let the steaks rest, Mark surveyed the table.

Steamed ears of sweet corn, potato salad, kale slaw, and chips with salsa. A late-summer feast to whet their appetites before cooler weather. Where Jackie found the sweet corn, he didn't know, but he was glad to have them. If there was one thing he'd learned about his girlfriend in the last four months, it was her resourcefulness.

"Is it time yet?" Jackie asked, pulling out her chair and taking her seat.

"Might as well be." Mark sat down opposite her at her kitchen table. He started to reach for a steak, his fork poised over the platter, but Jackie stopped him.

"Wait."

"What is it?" he asked.

"Let's have a toast to our new adventure," Jackie said.

Mark smiled, setting down the fork. "Okay, you do it then." He picked up his soda glass as Jackie did the same.

"To co-habitation."

Mark echoed the sentiment and added his own. "And, to Ms. Jackie Thorndike, a full-fledged graduate of the Northeast Culinary Institute Baking and Pastry Arts Program.

They clinked glasses before drinking.

"I can't believe they reversed their decision."

Mark leaned over and kissed her forehead. "You deserved to finish."

Staring into the soda glass, Mark frowned. "My brother is so happy to be rid of my sorry ass; he's probably drinking champagne right now."

"You don't want to start over again after six weeks of sobriety, do you?"

Shaking his head adamantly, Mark picked a cherry tomato off a salad and popped it in his mouth.

"It was a long six-week stay with your brother, wasn't it?" Jackie giggled. "How did you get him to let you stay so long?"

"Money talks with Joey. I offered him $300 rent to sleep in that stuffy loft." Mark chuckled. "He's going to miss that if not my ass now! I won't miss the temptation of his refrigerator full of beer."

They dug into their meal, eating with gusto after a hard day of work.

When they finished, they settled on the living room couch.

Suddenly Mark got up and retrieved something from the pocket of his jean jacket.

He handed her a small velvet jewelry box before sitting next to her.

Eyes wide and her voice catching in her throat, Jackie opened the box. Inside was a pair of pearl stud earrings. She covered her eyes with her forearm, head bowed, as she started to cry. "You remembered."

"Of course. We picked them out together, right?"

"You've held on to them? All these years?"

"Yup. I figure it's about time you got 'em. They were meant to be your graduation present when you finished the Baking and Pastry Arts Program. I'm sorry you had to wait eight years for them."

She reached across the table and took Mark's hand. "Thank you. I love them. They mean so very much."

"Good. Glad you like the gift. Don't be expecting 'em often."

Jackie gave his hand a squeeze. "I don't need gifts to know you love me."

Shades of red started to creep up Mark's neck to his cheeks. "Good. I don't need any to know you love me either. We understand each other perfectly."

Jackie shifted over and shimmied herself into his lap. "I know you're a big curmudgeon."

Mark smiled as he put his arms around her. "That's right. Don't you forget it," he said, pulling her closer. His lips met hers for a quick peck, but he went back for more. When they came up for air again, he said, "what do you say we try out that new bed."

"It's hardly new. It only has a few new pillows. Yours, I might add."

"Forget the technicality woman. Do you want to check out the bed or not?"

Jackie laughed as she stood up. "Yes, of course. Mr. Suave and Debonair."

She took his hand again to lead him down the hallway to the bedroom.

"Wait a minute." Mark searched through his duffel bag still in the center of the living room floor. He pulled something red out, went to the apartment door, and fiddled with the outside doorknob.

As he walked back toward her, her eyebrows scrunched together and she asked, "What did you do?"

"Joe said he might stop by." He grabbed her hand to lead her to the bedroom.

Curious, Jackie shook him off and pulled the door open to see what he'd done. A bright red bandanna was wrapped around the doorknob. She gave him a quizzical look.

Mark walked over, rolling his eyes, swooped her up in his arms and carried her to the bedroom.

<u>Acknowledgements</u>

At the risk of sounding like a looped recording, my mentors and supporters have my heartfelt thanks:

Valerie Lynne, an awesome writer and a wonderful critique partner and friend. I love how we get work done on Zoom, giggling along the way! Someday soon, I hope we can get back to meeting in person and commandeer that booth at the Warwick, RI Panera's again.

To my Betas, you know who you are! Your insights are always welcome and appreciated.

My outstanding editor, Lynne Pearson, who catches all my mistakes, and urges me on to make the story sparkle. You may be on the opposite coast, but you are near and dear in my heart.

To LPC: Ginger, Jackie, Debbie, and Patti. Your support for my dream warms my heart. Thank you for being the zaniest, most wonderful BFFs a girl could ever want! Love you all!

To my S.O., better known in my newsletters and blogs as "G." for putting up with my disappearing acts to the writing desk, soothing my temper tantrums when the computer isn't doing what I want it to, and for keeping me in a steady supply of love and wine. You are my hero!

BLOOMIN' IN LOVE

(To be released January 2022)

CHAPTER ONE

Regina Maxwell hurried across the parking lot toward the front entrance of the grocery store. With a lengthy list, she headed for the row of interlocked shopping carts. Grasping the handle of the end cart she pulled; her arm jerking nearly from her shoulder socket as the cart remained nestled with its long line of brethren. Gina tugged harder. Again, the cart only jostled its neighbor without disconnecting from it.

"Oh, for heaven's sake," Gina huffed as she resettled her purse strap on her shoulder, set both hands on the handle and gave it a yank. It refused to let go. Teeth clenched and heat rising throughout her body, she threw her purse down on the sidewalk and heaved with all her might. Nothing.

Realizing her cart was stuck to its nearest neighbor, she tried pulling with one hand while pushing the connected cart away with her other arm. Still no go.

Eyes glazed over seeing red, she stamped her foot, seized the carts, and tried to kick them apart with all her power. Suddenly, a voice came from behind her.

"Wait, let me get that for you."

A cold sweat broke out on her forehead as her stomach dropped. She knew that voice.

Turning, she came face to face with the man she'd known and left long ago – Tony Perret. From the look of his face, he was just as surprised to see her as she was to see him.

"Gina?" he asked, his arms dropping to his sides.

"Tony," she replied, unhanding the cart. "What are you doing here?"

"Running an errand for my mother," he said, looking sheepishly at her while shuffling his feet. "Your hair. I didn't recognize you."

They eyed at each other suspiciously.

Regina brushed back a lock of hair from her eyes. "Visiting Mom and Dad? The rich and famous Vermont Senator and his family are back in town?" She reached down and picked up her handbag.

"You could say that." Tony folded his arms across his chest and swayed back on his heels.

Her eyes narrowed as she scowled, looking him up and down. Clearly there was something he wasn't saying. She could see it in the stiffness of his body. Knowing she couldn't beat it out of him and perturbed he was going to cause her to be late for work she blurted out, "I got to go." She turned back toward the cart and pulled on the handle one last time as if by some magic it would cooperate this time. It didn't move.

"Let me—" Tony started to say but Gina cut him off.

"Never mind. A hand basket will do," she snapped, flinging the strap of her handbag over her shoulder. She stomped through the store's automatic sliding doors leaving Tony on the sidewalk.

Tony shook his head as he watched her go.

Regina glanced over her shoulder when she got into the store. "Don't follow me."

Tony threw both arms down at his sides, palms forward. "I wasn't planning to. Why would I?"

"Don't get smart with me, Edgar Anthony Perret," Gina bit back, pointing her index finger at him.

"Don't be so paranoid," Tony scoffed. "Look, why don't you just go about your shopping, and I'll come back later."

"Fine." Gina turned on her heels and scurrying into the nearest aisle. When she reached its safety, she peeped around the corner and watched through the window panes as Tony stalked to a pickup, got in, and drove away. Only then did she breathe again

More Books by Diana Rock

<u>Fulton River Falls Series</u>
Melt My Heart
Proof of Love
Bloomin' In Love
First Christmas Ornament
<u>Colby County Series</u>
Bid to Love
Courting Choices (Release date 10/20/2022)
<u>MovieStuds Series</u>
Hollywood Hotshot
Hollywood Hotdog (release 2023)

Diana Rock lives in eastern Connecticut with her tall, dark, and handsome hero, and one very spoiled elderly kitty.

She putters in the yard and gardens or cooks and bakes up a storm in the kitchen in her spare time. And she hopes to be reeling with the Royal Scottish Country Dance group again soon! You can sign up for her monthly newsletter and/or twice monthly blog post on her website: DianaRock.com

Don't miss out!

Visit the website below and you can sign up to receive emails whenever Diana Rock publishes a new book. There's no charge and no obligation.

https://books2read.com/r/B-A-YUKN-FTXRB

BOOKS 2 READ

Connecting independent readers to independent writers.

CPSIA information can be obtained
at www.ICGtesting.com
Printed in the USA
BVHW090125130922
646694BV00004B/24